They weren't real, McKenzie reminded herself for the dozenth time in the past five minutes.

Literally, she kept telling herself, because it was easy to forget they were pretending when Ryder smiled at her with a certain look in his eyes.

Ryder wasn't her boyfriend.

Despite her reminder, which had been for herself as much as for Ryder, he was smiling.

Why wouldn't he be? It didn't matter to him that they weren't real, that the sexual tension building between them on the dance floor was a by-product of proximity, pretense and young healthy bodies rather than something more.

Her family all bought that they were a real couple.

Only, rather than being happy at how well her plan was working, she laid her head back against his shoulder and moved to the music with him in slow rhythmic movements and fought sighing.

Because they were doing such a good job pretending that they were convincing her, too.

Dear Reader,

Have you ever traveled somewhere and thought, *I could live here*? That's what happened to me during my first trip to Seattle. Moving from Tennessee to Seattle wasn't exactly feasible for me, but for Dr. McKenzie Wilkes it made perfect sense. Thank goodness I get to live vicariously through her on her trip through Pike Place Market. Only, unlucky-at-love McKenzie gets dumped just weeks before having to go home to Tennessee for her cousin's wedding. Thank goodness there's yummy Dr. Ryder Andrews, who comes to her rescue.

McKenzie doesn't expect Ryder to do more than help her save face at her cousin's wedding, but when she discovers her fake boyfriend is more real than any man she's ever known, can she resist the lure of something much more than a weekend fling?

I hope you enjoy Ryder and McKenzie's story. I had so much fun visiting Seattle and writing this one. I love to hear from readers at janice@janicelynn.net.

Happy reading,

Janice

WEEKEND FLING WITH THE SURGEON

JANICE LYNN

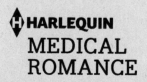

HARLEQUIN

MEDICAL
ROMANCE

HARLEQUIN®
MEDICAL
ROMANCE™

Recycling programs
for this product may
not exist in your area.

ISBN-13: 978-1-335-14963-3

Weekend Fling with the Surgeon

Copyright © 2020 by Janice Lynn

This edition published by arrangement with Harlequin Books S.A.

For questions and comments about the quality of this book,
please contact us at CustomerService@Harlequin.com.

Harlequin Enterprises ULC
22 Adelaide St. West, 40th Floor
Toronto, Ontario M5H 4E3, Canada
www.Harlequin.com

Printed in U.S.A.

USA TODAY and *Wall Street Journal* bestselling author **Janice Lynn** has a master's in nursing from Vanderbilt University and works as a nurse practitioner in a family practice. She lives in the southern United States with her Prince Charming, their children, their Maltese, named Halo, and a lot of unnamed dust bunnies that have moved in after she started her writing career. Readers can visit Janice via her website at janicelynn.net.

Books by Janice Lynn

Harlequin Medical Romance

Christmas in Manhattan

A Firefighter in Her Stocking

It Started at Christmas...
The Nurse's Baby Secret
The Doctor's Secret Son
A Surgeon to Heal Her Heart
Heart Surgeon to Single Dad
Friend, Fling, Forever?
A Nurse to Tame the ER Doc
The Nurse's One Night to Forever

Visit the Author Profile page
at Harlequin.com for more titles.

**Janice won the National Readers' Choice Award
for her first book,
The Doctor's Pregnancy Bombshell.**

To my bestie, Kimberly Duffy, for convincing me
I needed to visit Seattle.

CHAPTER ONE

DUMPED. HOW COULD Paul have dumped her?

Dr. McKenzie Wilkes stared at the phone message, not quite believing what she was reading.

Not just dumped, but via text. Seriously?

What did it say that Paul had dumped her via a typed message? That she hadn't warranted an in-person kick to the curb?

After more than two years of dating and his promise of undying love, she'd at the minimal deserved a call and explanation, surely? At least Clay, her ex prior to Paul, had broken things off in person rather than through technology.

To be fair, Paul had tried calling the previous evening.

Only she'd not seen the missed call until too late to dial back because she'd been on call at the hospital until six this morning and she'd been swamped. She'd not even seen the notification until long after midnight. Was this what he'd wanted to talk to her about? That he no longer loved her and wanted to end their relationship?

McKenzie bit the inside of her lower lip as she glared at the phone screen. Nope, she was not going to cry. Not going to happen. She had to go inside Seattle Cardiac Clinic for Kids and put on a happy face. How could she not when her patients and their families were dealing with so much more than a broken relationship?

Their sweet little hearts really were broken, physically as well as emotionally. Yet, most of her patients' families had amazing attitudes once the initial shock wore off. Yeah, she had to get her act together and not give in to the urge to go home, crawl into bed, curl into the fetal position and cry until there were no tears left.

Her patients needed her.

McKenzie loved her job as a pediatric cardiologist and advocate for her patients. She often got caught up in work, volunteering to take on extra shifts or canceling plans because one of her patients was in crisis.

She'd thought Paul had understood. Perhaps he hadn't. He worked for an online retailer. His clients didn't die if something went wrong.

McKenzie bit deeper into her lower lip, hoping the physical pain would defer the shattering in her chest.

Paul loved her. Hadn't he told her so hundreds, if not thousands, of times over the past two years? How could he just text that they needed time apart to reevaluate their feelings? That he felt they'd grown apart and had different life views and goals?

Pretty much all her future personal plans were tied up with Paul and the life they'd someday have together. She'd thought they'd be married within the next year or two, would start a family, would grow old together.

Then again, she'd thought the same thing with Clay, hadn't she? He'd ended a seven-year-long relationship that had begun during medical school and ended it when she'd thought they'd be taking that next life step together. Instead, he'd told her he was accepting a residency in Boston and she wasn't invited.

Oh, the pity she'd gotten at home following that breakup. As if dealing with her own inner misery wasn't enough, her mother had just about driven her crazy with date setups and poor-you babying.

She'd had to get away. Taking a residency offer in Seattle had been a godsend in so many ways.

Unfortunately, McKenzie was about to have an emotional déjà vu. A bad one. Possibly one worse than the last. In just under a month, she would be traveling to Tennessee for the first time since she'd moved.

For her cousin Reva's wedding with McKenzie as one of the bridesmaids. They'd always planned to be in each other's weddings. McKenzie had even wondered if Paul would use the trip to pop the question himself.

Obviously not.

Why had she hinted to her mother that a proposal might be in her near future? Wasn't that like throwing gasoline on a fire?

Going to Jeremy and Reva's wedding single was not an option. Her mother would feel it her obligation to push every Tom, Dick and Harry at her, all the while offering her looks of pity and conversations about how she'd once again been dumped.

McKenzie's fingers palmed the phone she held as reality further sank in. Paul had ended their relationship. He didn't love her anymore, if he ever had.

Sure, he'd never sent her heart into the acrobatics childhood fairytales had made her think were supposed to happen when she was around her significant other, but she enjoyed his company, their relationship made sense, and she genuinely cared for him. Besides, who believed in those kind of fairy tales, anyway?

Their relationship had been pleasant, comfortable, like warm cocoa on a cold drizzly Seattle night. Paul was dependable and made her happy.

She'd loved her cocoa guy. He'd made her feel loved, needed, as if she mattered.

"Hey, Dr. Wilkes," one of her colleagues called, jarring McKenzie to the fact that she was standing frozen to the spot where she'd gotten the text.

"Hi, back," she called, giving a little wave and

pretending that her world hadn't just crashed around her as she made her way inside the building and toward her office.

Her hands shook. Thank goodness she was in clinic today and not doing procedures where she had to have super steady hands.

It was more than her hands that shook.

Her entire body trembled.

Paul had dumped her.

Feeling a wave of lightheadedness hit her, McKenzie paused on her way to her office, leaned her forehead against the cold concrete wall, and closed her eyes.

She'd be okay. Even if Paul didn't love her anymore, she'd be fine. Somehow.

Even if she had to go to Reva's wedding and pretend everything was just lovely in her own life despite being single again, she'd survive those looks and conversations behind her back.

Her stomach knotted and sweat burst from her skin.

Oh, how her mother had gone on and on about how she looked forward to meeting Paul, how she couldn't wait to meet the man her daughter loved, planned to marry and start a family with.

Nausea pitched, rising up McKenzie's throat. A fresh wave of clamminess coated her skin.

She was going to throw up.

"Ahem."

At the deep clearing of a throat, McKenzie spun and almost lost her balance as she came face-to-face with Dr. Ryder Andrews.

Fire spread across her cheeks at the furrowing of his brows.

Ugh. Of all the people in the world to see her on the verge of being physically ill, why, why, why, had it had to be him?

The reality was, Ryder always sent her heart racing, jitters in her veins and a fluttery schoolgirl feel in her stomach. Ugh. She did not like how he made her feel. Even when things had been all flowery and friendly, he'd turned her insides all quivery. Then again, she was a fresh-out-of-residency pediatric cardiologist and he was a highly skilled pediatric heart surgeon.

Of course, she'd been a little in awe. She still was. That was only natural but had always made her feel a tad guilty.

If Paul was warm cocoa that made McKenzie feel warm and cozy inside, Ryder Andrews was 100-proof whiskey, leaving her off balance and fuzzyheaded.

Ryder was not comfortable. He was…concerned.

"Are you okay?"

Tears prickled. Could this day get worse? She just wanted to go home, restart her day. This time, without a dismissive text message and a run-in with her least-friendly coworker.

"Fine," she lied, because no way was she telling Ryder that she'd just been dumped.

He stared at her with his honey-colored eyes, rimmed with thick lashes, that, on the rare occasion their paths crossed, she avoided looking into because she felt as if he saw too much. Like now. Because she'd swear he knew she was lying.

Okay, she had been leaning against the wall and on the verge of losing her morning's coffee. It didn't take a genius IQ to realize she wasn't on her game.

Of all people to see her moment of weakness, why Ryder?

As brilliant as he was, as great a pediatric cardiothoracic surgeon as he was, McKenzie was positive he didn't like her. She wasn't sure she liked him. When he was around, she felt edgy, as if she was on the verge of saying or doing something stupid. She always seemed to, too. Possibly because she was so self-conscious.

She wasn't one who had to have everyone like her, but Ryder had been friendly in the beginning. He'd smiled and teased her. She'd really liked him. She'd thought they would be good friends. After just a couple of weeks of his being at the hospital, he'd done a complete about-face. He'd never been openly hostile, just went out of his way to avoid her except for when work absolutely demanded they interact.

These days, when their paths did cross, an underlying tension she didn't understand was always present. She couldn't recall having done anything to upset him, had even asked him about it once. He'd denied that anything was wrong but continued to avoid her. She'd started doing the same. Perhaps she was overly sensitive to his attitude change but being around him left her rattled.

Like now.

Looking into those intelligent eyes that probed beneath the surface made her think he already knew she'd been dumped, and he sympathized with Paul for being saddled with her for so long.

"You don't look fine," he unnecessarily pointed out. "Do I need to get you a glass of water or call someone?"

Yep. Her day just kept getting better and better.

"I'll be fine." Which was a more honest answer than her first one. She would, right? She'd survived her breakup with Clay, and she'd survive Paul ending things.

Because he no longer loved her.

Was she so unlovable that the men in her life always ended up walking away?

"If you'll excuse me," she continued, needing to escape from Ryder's curious gaze before she went full-blown waterworks. "I've got a few things to take care of before I start seeing patients."

Like going to her office and bawling her eyes out.

She walked away before Ryder could say anything more or before she did anything further embarrassing.

Dumped.

Again.

Ugh.

The back of her neck tingling as it often did around Ryder, McKenzie turned, found he stood exactly where she'd left him.

He'd not moved, just stared after her. His brows were drawn together, as if he was deep in thought and not pleasant ones.

Pursing her lips into a tight line, she shot Ryder a look of disgust at his gender, then, head held high, she retreated into her office.

McKenzie closed the door, leaned against it and gave in to the waterworks.

Dr. Ryder Andrews stared at McKenzie's closed office door and felt torn into a thousand directions.

Just walk away, he ordered himself.

She obviously does not want to talk to you about whatever is going on. He sure didn't need to talk to her about whatever was going on.

The less he had to do with Dr. McKenzie Wilkes the better.

Because, when they'd first met, he'd found himself rapidly falling for her. Once he'd discovered she was seriously involved with another man, he'd quickly put a stop to those feelings and avoided her as much as possible to prevent any reoccurrence of his fascination with her.

She'd been upset this morning. Very upset.

When she'd turned from where her head had been pressed against the wall, almost as if for support, her face had been pale, her eyes glassy, her expression almost sallow. As if she were ill.

Walk away, he repeated.

Only, he couldn't not check on her. He was a doctor. She obviously wasn't feeling well. He might do his best to avoid her, but what kind of person ignored when one of his colleagues was sick?

Going to their clinic's break area, he got a glass of water and a pack of crackers. Maybe she hadn't eaten anything that morning and just needed to get a little something in her stomach.

Maybe he was ignoring the obvious, that McKenzie had not been having a hypoglycemic attack in the clinic hallway.

Something more had been wrong than her needing food.

He'd do the right thing. He'd take her the water,

make sure she was physically okay, then go back to barely acknowledging her existence.

It's the same as he'd do for any coworker.

Only when he knocked on her closed office door, she didn't respond.

Walk away. Walk away. Walk away.

Why wasn't he walking away and just minding his own business?

"I brought a glass of water and some crackers for you," he told her through the door.

Although he hadn't realized it when they'd met, when he'd looked at her and felt something deep in his gut he'd never felt before, there had always been barriers between them.

No answer.

He knocked again.

Nothing.

He turned to leave. She obviously didn't want to talk to him. He'd done his duty, tried to show common courtesy by getting her a drink and the crackers and she'd not even had the same common courtesy to respond.

What if she hadn't been able to respond?

The question hit him hard, punching him in the gut, and stalling his feet. What if she'd gone into her office and something bad had happened?

She'd looked as if something was really wrong, had been leaning against the wall for support and been pale as a ghost. Had she gone into her office and passed out?

He knocked on the door again. This time brisker and with more urgency.

Nothing.

"McKenzie, open up." Because the more his brain raced, the more he knew he couldn't just walk away without making sure she was all right. He had to know she was okay even if it meant later being accused of overreacting.

Her office door could be locked. If so, he'd break in or get help.

"If you don't answer, I'm coming in to make sure you're not passed out on the floor."

What was Ryder's problem? McKenzie wondered as she lifted her head off her knees and tried to get her blurry eyes to focus on the room around her. He'd barely acknowledged she existed for months and today of all days he felt the need to make sure she wasn't passed out on the floor?

"Go away."

There. She'd answered. He could leave.

"I brought you water and crackers," he repeated.

"You can have them."

Water and crackers weren't going to solve her problems.

"I'm not going away until I make sure you're okay."

Ugh. If he was waiting on her to be okay, he might be there awhile.

She would be okay, she told herself again. Eventually. Hadn't she been after Clay had broken her heart? Sure, it had taken a long time and meeting and falling for Paul, but she had recovered from Clay's blow to her heart.

She had experience in recovering. This time shouldn't take nearly as long to get back on her feet, to make the pain in her chest go away, to not want to burst into tears at every sappy song on the radio.

Yeah, she was a pro at this getting dumped and would be shaking off Paul's wanting time apart. No big deal.

"I'm not leaving, McKenzie. Open up." He knocked on the door again.

Ugh. He was making so much commotion in the hallway he had to be drawing the attention of their colleagues. She could do without everyone there knowing she was Paul's yesterday news.

She stood from where she had been crouched on the floor, wiped her eyes, took a deep breath and told herself she had this. That Ryder was just a man. A gorgeous man who'd probably never been dumped, but, still, just a man.

She didn't bother forcing a smile to her face because she wanted him to know she didn't appreciate his concern. Perhaps she should, but at the moment she just wanted to wallow in her pity a few minutes.

"What is your problem?" she asked as she

flung the door open. Okay, so that hadn't been very nice of her, but he was seriously butting into her business and she just wanted to be left alone.

Seeming stunned by her irritation, he held the water and package of crackers out to her. "These are yours."

"Fine. I'll take them." She did just that, taking them from him. "You can go now."

"I... Okay, I will." He studied her face.

McKenzie lifted her chin, almost daring him to say something. Yes, she had been crying. Yes, she knew her eyes were swollen. Yes, it embarrassed her that he was seeing her this way.

"Is there anything I can do?" he surprised her by asking, deflating her false bravado.

"I... No, there's nothing you can do." Nothing anyone could do. Either Paul loved her and wanted to spend the rest of his life with her or he didn't. Embarrassed that Ryder was seeing her when she was so dejected, when she knew her eyes were red rimmed from crying and that she likely had mascara running down her cheeks, she forced a weak smile to her face. "I had a long night on call at the hospital and didn't get much rest. This morning has had a few unexpected things come up." To say the least. "Thank you for the water and crackers."

It was nice of him to get them for her when he hadn't had to. She must have looked really bad for him to have felt the need. If he'd wanted reassurance on that, she doubted she looked any better after her mini-boohoo-fest.

"Truly." She mentally willed the corners of her mouth upward again. "I'll be fine."

With that she closed the door, leaving him on the other side, and her knowing she had to get her act together to make it through the rest of her day.

If Ryder, who didn't even like her, had shown such pity, her friends would be holding an intervention.

She'd wash her face, repair her makeup, and, should anyone ask, she'd blame any remaining puffy redness on her hospital on-call shift. Tonight, in the privacy of her home, she'd give rein to her broken heart.

CHAPTER TWO

A WEEK HAD passed since Paul's decision to rock McKenzie's world. The feeling of being on the verge of constant tears had eased somewhat. Instead, a mounting sense of panic was rapidly taking its place.

In less than two weeks she had to go to Tennessee to be in her cousin's wedding.

Her cousin with the perfect life that her mother went on and on about. That was, when she wasn't going on and on about how much she looked forward to meeting McKenzie's future husband.

Because no matter how many times she'd attempted to tell her mother that she and Paul had broken up, McKenzie hadn't been able to drag the words from the pits of her being.

She didn't want to hear the sorrow, the pity, the disappointment in her mother's voice.

Nor had she been able to tell Reva.

Oh, how she and her cousin had been so close once upon a time. Just for the longest time McKenzie had sensed her cousin's awkwardness with McKenzie's unhappy personal life, her guilt that her own love life seemed to always be so perfect when McKenzie's hadn't. Until McKenzie had started dating Paul, she and Reva had reached the point of barely talking. Only over the past few months as McKenzie had convinced her cousin that, yes, she had her own perfect life in Seattle, had she and her cousin's relationship started getting past the awkwardness that had reared its ugly head when McKenzie had taken the residency in Seattle, despite all her family pushing her to stay in Nashville. Mostly, because they worried about her and wanted to fix her up with blind date after blind date.

No thank you.

Her mother had even gone online trying to find McKenzie dates in Seattle.

Meeting Paul and being able to tell her family to back off had been a godsend. Suddenly the tension between her and her mother had eased, the tension between her and Reva had eased.

Even McKenzie's brother had seemed less worried about her being so far away.

How could she tell them she'd been dumped again?

The pressure to move home would renew, the meddling in her love life—or lack thereof—would start again. You'd think being so far away would keep the damage at a minimum, but McKenzie knew better.

She couldn't go to Tennessee single.

Nor could she cancel out on being in Reva's wedding. If Reva ever found out her reasons for doing so, her cousin's guilt would be tenfold at having the perfect life while poor McKenzie had been dumped yet again.

Getting involved with someone was the last thing McKenzie wanted. Her breakup with Paul was too fresh. Maybe she'd never want to get involved again, but would decide to focus on her career and would dedicate her life to helping heal as many tiny hearts as she could even if she couldn't do a darned thing to repair her emotionally broken one.

McKenzie didn't want to meet anyone, didn't want to start a new relationship, didn't want the hassle of another heartbreak down the road.

Which explained her rather embarrassing internet search.

She was at the hospital in a small dictation room off the pediatric cardiology unit, waiting on test results on a new admit, and had let desperation take hold during the rare moment of downtime.

She scrolled through her search results for "reputable dating services." Ugh. How could she be so successful in her professional life and so unsuccessful in her personal?

This would cost her a small fortune but would be worth every penny to keep the focus on her cousin's wedding bliss and off McKenzie's latest heartbreak. She'd have to hire someone from Seattle to fly to Tennessee with her, rather than use a Nashville service. She couldn't risk her family bumping into a purchased date and knowing what she'd done. How embarrassing would that be?

Down the road, once they were past Reva's wedding and McKenzie was back in Seattle, she'd tell them the truth.

But to keep everyone happy and her own life a lot less stressful, McKenzie needed a wedding date pronto.

"I'm not sure I want to know."

Oh, flipping pancakes! Ryder!

Face going hot, McKenzie minimized the computer screen and wished she could hide her mortification as easily as she turned to face him.

He leaned against the doorjamb, his brows drawing together, and an odd look on his face. "Did something happen to you and the guy you've been seeing?"

What was he doing there? Okay, so she was at the hospital in the dictation area, but had he forgotten he didn't like her and kept his distance?

Too bad he hadn't avoided her just now.

"You could say that," she admitted, taking a deep breath and not meeting Ryder's intent gaze. Maybe if she didn't look directly at him, he wouldn't see how horrified she was that he'd caught her looking at escort services. Desperate times called for desperate measures.

"I thought you two were long-term." He studied her as if he was trying to solve some great mystery.

McKenzie sighed. He'd already caught her looking at dating agencies, had seen her raccoon-eyed last week. What more could it hurt to admit she'd been dumped? She could hide the truth for only so long before word got out among her co-workers, anyway.

"We were, only now, we're not." She shrugged as if it wasn't a big deal. As if she hadn't spent the last week trying to figure out what it was about her that eventually always drove away the men in her life.

"Good riddance. He wasn't right for you."

McKenzie's jaw dropped at Ryder's unexpected and rather forceful comment. The two men had met only a couple of times and had never had a conversation as far as she knew. Why would Ryder have thought Paul wrong for her?

"Paul is a nice man. I will win him back," she murmured, then blushed when she realized she'd made the claim out loud. Why had she? Yes, she was distraught at the breakup, cared for Paul and had thought they'd marry, but win him back? They'd barely spoken since his devastating text.

"You weren't the one to end the relationship?" Disbelief filled Ryder's voice.

Yeah, right. McKenzie had never been the one to end a relationship. Not ever.

Ryder had straightened from the doorjamb, had moved further into the tiny room.

McKenzie's heart rate sped up and she swallowed as she stared up at him.

She wished she could just disappear. Poof. Be gone.

Ryder gestured to the computer where he'd seen her search results. "Are you planning to try to make him jealous?"

She glanced at the screen, no longer lit with her escort service search. She hadn't, but his thinking that was better than his knowing the truth. "Do you think it would work?"

Maybe if Paul thought she was moving on he'd come to his senses, realize he didn't want to lose her, and they could get back to their normally scheduled lives.

Ryder's dark brow lifted. "Is that really what you're doing? Hiring a date to make your ex jealous?"

Ugh. She sounded pathetic. Would admitting the truth, that she needed a date for her cousin's wedding be more, or less, pathetic?

"It's really none of your business," she reminded him, then blurted out something so crazy she couldn't believe she'd said it. "Unless you'd like to make it your business by being my boyfriend for a weekend?"

Ryder never sought McKenzie out. Never.

But he hadn't been able to get her sad eyes out of his mind no matter how he tried.

Which explained why he'd hung around the hospital despite that he'd just finished checking his last patient consult that evening. Normally, he'd have taken off to make sure his path didn't cross with McKenzie's when he knew she was at the hospital.

Tonight, when he'd spotted her in the dictation room on his way out, he'd been drawn to her, meaning to just walk by and get a glimpse, maybe say hi and assure his mind that she was, indeed, fine as she'd claimed so that maybe, just maybe, her tear-streaked face would quit haunting him.

Not since finding out she was taken had she occupied so much of his mind. Prior to that, he'd thought about her almost constantly.

The past week he'd reverted to doing so again and hadn't liked it.

You knew something had upset her, he reminded himself. Had told himself she'd probably had to give bad news to a family during her hospital shift and that had been what upset her. Lord knew there were times when doing so gutted him enough that he fought tears.

The thought that something personal might have caused her tears had crossed his mind, but he'd dismissed it. Even if McKenzie and her man were having issues, the last thing Ryder wanted was to be a rebound guy.

Been there, done that, had the scars to prove it.

"You want to use me to make your ex jealous?"

"Maybe," she surprised him by admitting. "Are you seeing anyone?"

"No, but—"

"Look," she interrupted. "I'm not hitting on you. Nor do I want to date you," she clarified. Her tone conveyed that she found the idea preposterous. "Not for real. I just need someone to go with me to my cousin's wedding. Someone who won't take things wrong or have any relationship expectations and if Paul gets jealous in the process…" She shrugged.

McKenzie wanted to use him.

"I don't think it fair to invite someone who might get the wrong idea," she continued, perhaps to fill the silence as words failed Ryder.

He liked to think he rolled with the punches, but McKenzie asking him to be her pretend boyfriend for a weekend had him speechless.

"I'm not interested in replacing Paul." She took a deep breath. "But going to my cousin's wedding alone isn't a viable option."

The desperation that must have driven her to ask him to go with her kept Ryder from walking away.

Not that he'd say yes.

Her suggestion was ridiculous. Playing McKenzie's pretend boyfriend appealed about as much as the thought of torture.

His gaze narrowed. "When is the wedding?"

"Not this weekend, but next." At his widened eyes, she rushed on, "Short notice, I know."

"You want me to go with you to a wedding next weekend? As a pretend date? No strings attached?"

If not for her serious expression, he'd think she was pranking him.

"Want is such a mild word. I'll gladly repay the favor."

Ryder arched his brow. "You mean when I need someone to pretend to be my girlfriend?"

"Please say yes. I'm desperate." She pointed at the computer screen, reminding him of her escort service search. "Obviously."

"Being a pretend boyfriend for a wedding isn't on my bucket list. Sorry."

Her disappointment had him momentarily reconsidering, then he shook off the notion of saying yes just to ease the desperation in her big green eyes.

Once upon a time he'd have loved the excuse to spend time with her. Fortunately, he'd put that behind him.

Just as he planned to put this conversation behind him.

God, please let Ryder go back to avoiding her, McKenzie prayed. Because she was absolutely mortified at her blurted plea.

Had aliens taken over her brain? How could she have asked him something so insane?

Desperation really had turned McKenzie's mind to mush.

Ryder didn't even like her, so the very idea of his going with her was ridiculous.

No more ridiculous than hiring an escort service.

She dug her fingertips into her clammy palms.

At least she knew Ryder. He wouldn't get the wrong idea or be some criminal who'd slipped through the company's background checks.

She raked her gaze over his six-foot frame. Chestnut hair, strong nose and cheekbones, honey-colored eyes, dark, thick lashes, full lips framed by deep dimples. Ryder was gorgeous.

She'd thought it the day they met, and that hadn't changed with time.

Of course, Mr. Gorgeous had said no. He avoided her like the plague. Why would he bail her out of an unpleasant situation?

Only why was he still standing in the doorway?

He'd said no. Okay, fine. He should go away and let her get back to her internet search before she was notified regarding her new patient's test results.

"I didn't expect you to say yes." *Shut up, McKenzie.* "I mean, why would you go to Nashville with me?"

He blinked. "You wanted me to go to a wedding with you in Nashville, as in Tennessee?"

Yeah, that was a long way away from Seattle.

Nineteen hundred and seventy-four miles by plane.

Oh, how she knew every long torturous mile of that five-hour flight and how she dreaded every moment.

Just thinking of it had her heart flip-flopping.

Or maybe it was the way Ryder was looking at her that had triggered her cardiac acrobatics.

Perhaps he didn't like flying any more than she did.

"I would have paid your way," she defended, just in case he'd thought she'd meant for him to dig into his own pockets to help her.

He looked insulted and gestured toward her darkened computer screen. "I'm not for hire."

Her face heated. "That's not what I meant. My covering your expenses would only have been fair. You shouldn't have to pay to bail me out of a bad situation."

His expression became pensive. "Is that what this is? A bad situation?"

The worst.

"Spending the weekend with my family will be torture if I go home alone." For so many reasons. "They'll be beside themselves with worry that Paul and I've broken up. The last thing I want is to have everyone focused on my broken heart instead of my cousin's happy day." She sighed. "Plus, I'm in the wedding. I have to go. Yeehaw."

Feeling tears she'd have sworn she didn't have left fill her eyes, McKenzie turned toward the computer. She moved the computer mouse, lighting up the screen again.

"I just want to go home, celebrate my cousin's wedding and enjoy spending time with my family." A tall order, under the best of circumstances and perhaps impossible while trying to forget about her breakup with Paul. "But, no worries, I have a plan."

Not necessarily a great plan, but one that would hopefully suffice to keep her first trip home in eons from being completely ruined.

Maybe it would work.

Were those tears in McKenzie's eyes?

He'd stopped by the dictation room because he'd wanted to assure himself she was okay. Not to cause fresh tears in her beautiful eyes.

Which was what he'd managed to do.

He should have just kept walking, kept with the status quo of going the opposite direction when she was near.

But he hadn't. Now how was he supposed to quit being haunted by memories of her tears when he had another reminder?

When he'd triggered her tears with his prying?

Seeing her upset undid his insides, made him feel as if he'd wronged her by saying no.

McKenzie's breakup with Paul wasn't his problem.

Her trip home wasn't his problem.

So, why were his feet refusing to walk away?

Why was he wondering how difficult it would be to rearrange his hospital and clinic schedules?

"You're sure hiring a date for a weekend away is safe?"

Because he did not like the idea of a hired stranger being with her for an entire weekend.

Without turning to look at him, she shrugged. "It's not something that I've any experience with, but I plan to do my homework prior to finalizing which company and escort I go with."

Ignoring that he still stood there, she pulled out her cell phone and dialed a number from the computer screen.

"Hello? I'd like to make an appointment to possibly hire a date for next weekend." Pause. "Yes, for the entire weekend. If I decide to go with your company, it'll involve being with me around the clock and traveling out-of-state."

Hearing her say the words out loud, hearing the break in her voice, the resigned desperation but determination to proceed with this crazy idea of hers in her tone, left Ryder's insides cold.

He couldn't let her do it.

No way could he walk away and leave her at

the mercy of whomever the agency set her up with. What if the guy exploited her vulnerability? Or was a serial killer?

Ryder didn't consider himself any sort of a white knight, but his mother had raised him better than to stand by and watch a woman set herself up to be taken advantage of.

Nope. Not happening.

Walking over to her, heart pounding at what he was about to do, he took the phone from her and disconnected the call.

"Hey!" she fussed, reaching for her phone back. "What did you do that for?"

Hoping he didn't live to regret what he was about to agree to, Ryder handed over her phone. "You're not hiring someone to take you."

Her chin lifted. "Excuse me? I'm a grown woman and can do whatever I choose."

Ryder admired the flash of fire in her green gaze. "Sorry. I should rephrase that."

He took a deep breath, assured himself that he was doing only what any decent person would do, that he had no residual feelings for McKenzie, and that he was completely safe from falling under her spell again because he didn't do rebound relationships.

No getting involved with someone who was already emotionally involved with someone else, whether that was an active relationship, or one recently ended.

Not ever.

He'd go, keep her from possibly risking her safety by hiring a date, pretend to be her boyfriend to keep from spoiling her trip to Tennessee then he'd come home, and they'd go back to ignoring that they even knew each other.

"You don't need to hire anyone—" here went everything "—because I'll go with you to Nashville."

McKenzie couldn't have heard Ryder correctly. Had he really just said he'd go with her?

"I'll need details."

Hands shaking as she gripped the phone, he'd given her back, McKenzie couldn't hide her shock. "You'll go."

"If it means not having to worry about you traveling with a date you know nothing about—" his tone said that she'd been willing to do so was ludicrous "—then, yes, I'll go."

Disbelief filled her.

"Why?" She wasn't sure if she meant why would he worry about her or why would he be willing to go. Both, she decided. She didn't understand his reasons for either.

"Quit looking a gift horse in the mouth, McKenzie." He gave a low laugh, as if this wasn't anything out of the ordinary and she was making a big deal out of nothing. "Just tell me what I need to know so I can get my schedule rearranged."

Because he was going to go with her.

He'd save her face regarding her breakup with Paul, ease any uncertainties her family had regarding her not being happy in Seattle and regarding Reva being the first to marry and McKenzie's suddenly single status. His being there would keep her family from playing pity party and matchmaker.

It could work.

"I'm flying in on Thursday—" saying the word *flying* had her stomach lurching "—so I can be there for the rehearsal on Friday and whatever else my cousin has planned. If you're sure—" she couldn't believe he was "—then, I'll purchase a ticket for you to fly up on Friday afternoon and to leave after the wedding on Saturday night."

"Is Saturday night when you're coming home?"

She shook her head. "I'm not headed back until Sunday."

Regarding her, Ryder shrugged. "I'll take off a few days, go with you on Thursday, and fly back with you on Sunday evening. I'm overdue a minivacation."

She'd never expected him to say yes, much less rearrange his work hours to accommodate her trip.

"Where will you stay?" She blurted the question without thought, much as she had her initially asking him to go with her. She especially hadn't considered how his next words would turn her insides outward.

"Wherever you are, *girlfriend.*"

Girlfriend? McKenzie's eyes widened and her teeth sank into her lower lip. *Hello, crazy heart rhythm.*

Heaven help her.

Her stomach flip-flopped much as it did at the thought of boarding a plane and being trapped inside for hours on end.

His answer shouldn't send her into panic mode.

His intent eyes shouldn't have her heart racing.

But they did. Maybe she hadn't thought this out as well as she should have.

Ryder was an attractive man. Perhaps she shouldn't toy around with dating him, not even when it wasn't real.

"I'm staying at my mom's."

"Fine. I'll stay there. I can sleep on the sofa, if needed." He didn't look concerned. "Unless you think your mother isn't going to like me and will throw me out?"

He was going. Never in a million years would she have thought he'd be who rescued her.

"My mother would like any man who was keeping me from spinsterhood."

It was the truth, but even the pickiest of mothers would leap for joy if their daughter brought home Dr. Ryder Andrews, pediatric cardiothoracic surgeon extraordinaire and gorgeous to boot.

"Spinsterhood?" Ryder's brow arched. "Your breakup with computer guy doesn't catapult you into fear of spinsterhood, surely?"

"You'd think, but try explaining that to my mother."

"If you want me to."

Because he'd be in Tennessee and would meet her mother. Something none of her Seattle friends had ever done, including Paul.

Had she not been so afraid to fly, they'd have gone home to meet her family. Her brother, Mark, had been to Seattle several times and seemed to like Paul well enough. Funny how childhood tragedy could leave one child terrified to board a plane and have another facing his past by becoming a pilot.

"You're really going to Tennessee?" she asked, wanting to make sure she wasn't misinterpreting. "That is what you're saying? You're going to pretend to be my boyfriend for my cousin's wedding weekend, so my family won't start using spinster hashtags when discussing me and I can enjoy my trip home without their pity or matchmaking?"

CHAPTER THREE

DR. RYDER ANDREWS didn't think McKenzie had anything to worry about when it came to spinster hashtags.

She was an intelligent, beautiful woman any man would be lucky to spend time with and call his own.

No doubt, when she was ready, she'd soon replace her ex.

But next weekend, she'd be spending with him.

With him playing the role of her pretend boyfriend.

He stared down into the wide green eyes looking up at him, full of hope that he was saying yes. Eyes he'd been avoiding looking into for months because he'd instantly liked McKenzie, been attracted to her, and quickly learned she was taken.

With McKenzie, he'd been tempted to walk down that slippery slope and risk the fallout.

He'd been down that road before, and it hadn't ended well.

That he was tempted to become involved with someone involved with someone else had made him that much more determined to stay away from her as much as possible.

He'd found her eyes enchanting, found looking into them left him unsettled, so he'd stayed away.

Yeah, McKenzie had no worries on growing old alone unless remaining single was what she chose. Not with those killer eyes that flashed with intelligence, lush auburn hair that he'd once thought about running his fingers through more often than he could count when his eyes closed and dreams took over, and a curvy bod that no lab coat or scrubs could conceal. He might have suppressed his fascination with her, but that didn't mean he didn't recognize that McKenzie was a beautiful woman.

If Ryder had to say what he liked best about her, though, his answer would be her intelligence and how she could see outside the box. How, during those first few weeks they'd known each other, their gazes could meet, and he'd know what she was thinking. She'd know what he was thinking. And they'd share a smile. When he'd realized she was off limits, he'd tried to avoid consults on her patients, but when it had been unavoidable, he'd always been impressed.

He'd never met anyone like her, had been disappointed she was already taken, had often had to remind himself to back away and remain aloof so as not to overstep.

He'd asked her once, early on, if she was happy in her relationship. She'd enthusiastically told him she was, that she and Paul were in love and planned to spend the rest of their lives together.

That's when he'd decided to squash his attraction to her.

"I've never been to Nashville," he admitted, knowing she was waiting for him to clarify that he was going. "Maybe we'll get a chance to do a little sightseeing."

"Seriously?" Her forehead scrunched. "You're going with me and will be my pretend boyfriend?"

Rather than see her hire an escort service? Absolutely.

"I'll go with you to your cousin's wedding in Tennessee as your pretend boyfriend."

McKenzie asking Ryder to be her pretend boyfriend had morphed him into the friendly man she'd met initially.

Okay, not quite that friendly, but he at least didn't run in the opposite direction anymore when he spotted her.

Whether at the clinic or at the hospital, he'd smile when their paths crossed, had even stopped to chat when he'd come into the break room and found McKenzie and her nurse there, having coffee while discussing phone calls from patients' parents.

He'd stuck around only long enough to refill

his reusable water bottle, but his smile had stuck with her for the remainder of the day.

As long as he was smiling, that meant he hadn't changed his mind, right?

Regardless, his avoidance of her seemed to be a thing of the past.

Such as now with Sawyer Little's case.

McKenzie had been doing her one day a week on call at the hospital when she'd been consulted for the newborn who'd been okay for the first few hours of life but had started having a grayish-blue tinge to her skin—thankfully her mother had noticed and called for the nurse.

The nurse noted a decreased oxygen level and mild dyspnea and contacted the pediatrician. The pediatrician had checked the baby, ordered an oxygen tent and consulted McKenzie as he suspected a cardiac issue in the newborn.

McKenzie was just getting ready to do a cribside echocardiogram when Ryder had walked into the neonatal cardiac intensive care unit.

Meeting her gaze, his eyes darkened, but then, the corners of his mouth lifted.

Heaven help her, the man had an amazing smile.

That had to be why her breath hitched up a few notches.

An alarm dinged from the next bay over and it took McKenzie a moment to realize it hadn't been a warning bell sounding in her own head.

She really needed to keep Ryder in proper perspective. She was just getting out of her relationship with Paul. The last thing she needed was to confuse Ryder's kindness with the possibility of something more happening between them.

She didn't want anything more to happen between them.

The nurse who was assisting McKenzie with Sawyer glanced up. "That's my other patient. I need to change an intravenous medication bag."

"Go," McKenzie told the woman. Each NICU nurse was assigned two patients, typically. "I'm good and will call out if I need you for anything."

The nurse took off for the next bay. Their unit was designed with an open hallway with each baby in their own semiprivate three-sided bay. The nurse's station was on the opposite side of the hallway and faced the open bays.

Ryder had stopped at the nurses' station and was pulling up a chart on the computer system. He wore dark navy scrubs and she doubted anyone would be surprised if a camera crew walked in and started filming his every move for some medical drama. He looked as if he should be gracing the big screen and tugging on hearts by resolving one medical drama after another.

McKenzie pulled her attention back to the sweet little girl, took warmed gel, tested the temperature on the back of her hand, then applied some to Sawyer's chest.

She ran the conducer over the baby's left ribs, checking the heart chambers, walls, valves and vessels.

She grimaced at what she found.

Sawyer's left ventricle and aorta were too small. There was very little blood flow through the underdeveloped left side of the heart, which explained the faint bluish tinge to the baby's skin despite the oxygen her pediatrician had started.

"You have a minute?" she called over to where Ryder stood fifteen or so feet away.

"Sure." First making a couple of clicks to close out whatever he'd been looking at on the screen, he came into the bay and stood by Sawyer's hospital bed. "Everything okay?"

"Not for this little one. She was born during the night. Mom attempted her first breastfeeding and thought her color looked off. Her pediatrician consulted me. Unfortunately, I'm going to be consulting a pediatric cardiothoracic surgeon and you just happened to be standing nearby."

Ryder glanced down at the almost seven-pound baby with various tubes and monitors attached. McKenzie moved the conducer back over the baby's chest to show Ryder the undersized ventricle and vessel and the lack of blood flow on the left side of Sawyer's heart.

"Hypoplastic left heart syndrome," Ryder said, giving voice to McKenzie's thoughts.

She nodded. "It wasn't picked up on during

Mom's ultrasound. She only had one, between four and five months, but the anomaly mustn't have been as prominent as Mom says nothing unusual was mentioned."

McKenzie moved the conducer over to where she could see the ductus arteriosus. The small vessel that connected the aorta to a pulmonary artery was still patent, allowing oxygenated blood to travel from the right ventricle to the aorta. Thank goodness.

If the opening closed, as it normally did within a couple of days, blood wouldn't be able to be pumped to the body.

If blood wasn't being pumped to her body, Sawyer would die.

"Is she on Prostaglandin E1?"

"Not yet," McKenzie answered, knowing they needed to start the substance that the body naturally made to keep the vessel open while in utero, but that the body stopped making at birth. "She'd just started showing symptoms right before I was consulted and you're seeing this as I am."

"Gotcha. I'll get an order for stat Prostaglandin E1 so we can keep that vessel open," Ryder offered, walking over and logging into the bay's computer to type in the order.

The nurse came back into Sawyer's bay and Ryder told her what he'd ordered.

The nurse nodded, then went to carry out the order to start the medication that would, hopefully, prevent Sawyer's ductus arteriosus from closing.

"It's on its way," he assured her, watching as McKenzie still checked the baby with the ultrasound machine.

"Look at the foramen ovale." She pointed out the hole between Sawyer's heart ventricles. "It's patent, but what do you think?"

She let him take the ultrasound conducer so he could run it over the baby's chest to get the views he wanted. He did so, studying what he saw.

"The opening is too small," he yet again verbalized what she'd been thinking.

"She'll need to go to surgery as soon as I can get her on schedule."

"Yes," Ryder agreed. "Her oxygen level is running low enough even with her oxygen mask that you're going to need to put her on a ventilator as well to keep her from getting into trouble."

McKenzie nodded. "Poor little sweetheart has a long road ahead of her."

"Yes, she does, but a road that's smoother than it used to be."

Something in his voice had McKenzie lifting her gaze from the baby to stare at him.

He had an expression she'd never seen on him in the past, one that hinted his mind had gone somewhere far beyond the pediatric cardiac care unit where they were.

Was he thinking about the research he was involved with?

Ryder belonged to a research team involved in 3D printing of human cardiac tissue research that hoped to eventually be able to use the printed tissue for surgical rebuilding of too-small aortas and to repair other congenital heart anomalies, among other heart repairs.

Not long after they'd met he'd told her the research opportunities had been what led his move to Seattle, that the development of 3D-printed cardiac tissue opened the doorway to great advances and better outcomes of the care they provided their patients, and he'd wanted to be a part of that research.

Was he wishing they were further along so Sawyer could benefit from the research being done at Trevane Technologies?

Or had something else caused the odd look on his face?

"Do you want me to consult one of the other surgeons?"

Seeming to snap out of whatever had momentarily taken hold, he shook his head. "Why would you do that when I'm already familiar with her case?"

"I just thought…" She paused, not sure whether to remind him that prior to a few days before he'd gone out of his way not to share patients with her, that her patients were always assigned to one of his colleagues, but never him. "If you're willing to take on her case, that would be wonderful."

"I'm willing," he assured her as he pulled out his phone and punched in a number. "Oddly enough, I've a Glenn shunt scheduled later this morning on a five-month-old."

McKenzie's brow lifted. Fortunately, they didn't see many hypoplastic left heart syndrome cases, so to diagnose a new one, especially one not picked up on during ultrasound, and Ryder to be doing surgery on another on the same day was indeed a coincidence.

The Glenn shunt was the second phase of the series of surgeries Sawyer would need on her heart. Usually that procedure occurred four to five months after the Norwood, the procedure that would connect the superior vena cava, which brought blood back to the heart from the upper half of the body to the pulmonary arteries to the head and then the lungs to be reoxygenated.

Later, a third surgery called a Fontan procedure would be needed when Sawyer was a toddler. The Fontan would connect her inferior vena cava, which was a big vein that brought the blood from her lower body to her heart, to her pulmonary arteries. Hopefully, at that point, Sawyer would do well and have normal oxygenation of her blood.

Ryder spoke to his nurse practitioner, telling her what he needed so she could handle getting the procedure scheduled. When he finished, he turned back to where McKenzie had told the nurse to gather what she'd need to ventilate the baby.

"I'll make sure Sawyer's Norwood procedure is done prior to our leaving for Nashville. I'll plan to do the surgery but will consult with Dr. Rhea—" another pediatric cardiothoracic surgeon at the hospital "—as he'll be covering my patients while I'm out of town."

"Thank you." She wasn't sure if she meant his taking on Sawyer's case and making sure the baby's surgery happened as soon as possible or if she was thanking him for being willing to shuffle his schedule to go with her to Nashville.

She appreciated both.

"It's my job," he reminded her, seeming almost embarrassed at her gratitude.

It was more than a job. For both of them.

That was one thing they had in common and she could always use as a go-to if they ran out of things to talk about on their trip. They both loved their job, doing what they could to repair tiny hearts, and save lives.

She hoped silence didn't abound because she didn't want to bore Ryder out of his mind.

"Do you want me to go with you to talk to this little one's parents?"

McKenzie's heart squeezed at the thought of what she'd soon be doing. Talking to new parents, explaining what was going on with their precious baby had always been McKenzie's least favorite part of her job.

"Thanks, but I'll tell them what's going on." She wouldn't pass that off on Ryder. She was Sawyer's pediatric cardiologist and needed to meet her mom and dad as they'd be seeing each other many times in the years to come. No doubt Ryder would meet with them soon enough to discuss specifics of the surgery. "Mom was who first picked up on something not being right, so she knows something's up. I'll spend some time explaining the diagnosis and what to expect. You can meet with them later when they've had a bit of time for the reality of what Sawyer faces to sink in."

Because the diagnosis, the stark reality of just how serious the diagnosis was, would put the child's parents into shock—they'd need a little time before they'd be able to process what was happening. It wasn't easy to go from thinking you had a healthy newborn to discovering that without major intervention she'd be dead within a few days.

His gaze met hers. "Do you want to assist?"

Be a part of his team to rebuild Sawyer's aorta? Was that a trick question?

"Absolutely."

"Awesome." His eyes sparkled, conveying he

was glad she'd said yes to going into surgery with him.

McKenzie's insides tingled at the way he was looking at her, at the fact he'd just asked her to be a part of his team.

Over the past year, she'd been a part of a few teams he led. Each time, she'd been impressed with his focus and skills as he intricately worked to repair whatever anomaly ailed their tiny patient.

He was such a talented surgeon and always seemed to go above and beyond in the care he provided.

She'd been so excited when he'd first come to work for Seattle Cardiac Clinic for Kids, had hoped to frequently go into surgery with him because of his involvement with several innovative techniques, including his research position. She'd thought about applying for a position on his research team, even.

Those first few weeks, she had been lucky enough to assist with a handful. And what seemed to be only another handful since that time.

Because he'd become almost inaccessible to her, and Dr. Rhea tended to see the majority of her patients.

Maybe she had done something to upset Ryder, she thought for the thousandth time. Whatever, he must have moved past it when she'd asked him to go with her to Nashville. She still couldn't imagine what she'd done, but obviously she had done something as he'd actively avoided her.

Whatever, he wasn't avoiding her anymore and had asked her to assist on Sawyer's Norwood procedure. Plus, he was smiling at her as he hit a button on his phone, making another call to set the wheels into motion to get Sawyer to surgery and to have McKenzie in the operating room with him, along with all the others who would be a part of Sawyer's heart surgery.

Going to surgery with him shouldn't make her so excited, but she'd be lying if she didn't admit that it did. She never wanted any child to be born with defects, but she loved every opportunity to help those who had been.

McKenzie brushed her fingertip gently over the baby's chest and said a quick prayer that everything would go smoothly during this first surgery, and the many more Sawyer would face during her lifetime. Two within her first six months.

It was highly possible that down the road, in addition to all her initial surgeries, that if a heart could be found, Sawyer would need a heart transplant.

If Sawyer survived her first year of life, her odds were good. Unfortunately, the number of babies who didn't survive was still too high.

Ryder's hand covered hers. "You sure you don't want me to go with you?"

Surprised at his touch, at the electricity that

shot up her arm, McKenzie met his gaze, marveling at the compassion she saw there, as if he understood all too well the devastation she was about to unleash upon the Littles.

"I... Thank you. That would be wonderful."

Why had Ryder offered to go with her to tell Sawyer's parents their precious baby had hypoplastic left heart syndrome and their lives would never be as they'd thought when they'd arrived at the hospital expecting to bring home a healthy baby?

Typically, by the point he interacted with a baby's parents they already had a good idea of what was going on. The Littles didn't.

But he'd seen the heaviness on McKenzie's heart at the prospect of going to talk to the baby's parents. What was it about her that had him yet again offering to jump to the rescue?

Ryder watched as McKenzie told the baby's upset family why they'd noticed the blue tinge to Sawyer's skin. Seeing how she patiently explained the problems with Sawyer's heart, answering their questions, and even drawing a simple visual of a normal heart and a likeness of Sawyer's, impressed Ryder with her compassion and thoroughness.

It also brought back memories.

Memories that he'd been too young to really understand at the time.

Memories that had changed his life.

Memories he relived every time he went into surgery, knowing his actions and a whole lot of divine intervention determined whether another family would go through what his once had.

"This is Dr. Ryder Andrews. He's a pediatric cardiothoracic surgeon and I consulted with him on your daughter's case. He examined her with me, saw what I saw on the ultrasound of Sawyer's heart. I know this is a lot to take in, but time is of the essence and decisions have to be made.

"I'm going to let him explain his recommendations, and then we'll discuss how you want to proceed."

As McKenzie had, Ryder explained what was needed for Sawyer to survive, he laid out the staggering obstacles that stood in her way, and the different options on tackling those obstacles.

He also gave the less-than-stellar statistics Sawyer faced, even with surgery.

"She'll die if you don't operate? You're sure?"

"Positive. Without a way to get oxygenated blood to her body, she has zero chance of survival. Even with surgery, she might not make it." He referred to the statistics he'd given them with each phase of treatment. "It's up to you on how we proceed. You can choose not to operate if that's what you both want."

"But she'd die!" Sawyer's mother sobbed, triggering her husband to wrap his arms around her.

"With surgery Sawyer faces a lifetime of health

challenges, but she does have a good chance of surviving and eventually having a somewhat normal life," McKenzie informed them, reaching over to place her hand on the woman's arm. "The decision is yours. If you need some time alone to discuss it, we can step out for a few minutes."

Sawyer's parents both shook their heads.

"We don't need more time," her father said, hugging his wife tighter.

"Operate," they said simultaneously.

Ryder explained what would happen over the next few days.

Not surprising to him, McKenzie hugged them, assuring she would keep them informed each step along the way.

Ryder shook their hands. As he was getting ready to move away, Sawyer's mother grasped his hand.

Tears ran down her face as her gaze met his. "Please save our baby girl."

Sharp pains stabbed into Ryder's chest. "I'll do my best."

The woman nodded. "Thank you."

"I—I know it's not much, but I do somewhat understand what you're feeling." He took a deep breath. "Over twenty years ago, my sister was born with the same condition Sawyer has." Ryder swallowed back the emotions that hit him when he recalled the turmoil his parents had gone through following Chrissy's birth. The same hell Sawyer's parents faced.

Only Ryder would do everything within his power to make sure Sawyer had a very different outcome from his sister.

"Did she survive?"

Ryder could feel McKenzie's gaze boring into him but didn't look her way. Couldn't look her way.

Wishing he'd kept his past to himself, Ryder kept his focus on the Littles and shook his head. "Technology was very different a quarter of a century ago. Babies with hypoplastic left heart syndrome rarely survived. That isn't the case now. Although there's still a chance Sawyer won't survive, odds are in her favor that she will."

Ryder talked with them for a few more minutes, then he and McKenzie left the obstetrics room Sawyer's mother was still in.

They walked in silence down the hallway to the elevator. Once inside, McKenzie's gaze lifted to his and was full of such emotions it threatened to overflow the elevator car.

"Oh, Ryder," she said with a sigh. "I'm so sorry about your sister."

"Me, too."

"Sometimes our job is so heart wrenching and I wonder why we do this," she mused.

"Not me. I've always known I'd specialize in pediatric cardiology."

Her look was full of empathy. "Because of your sister?"

"Yes," he answered, wishing they weren't having this conversation in an elevator.

Wishing they weren't having this conversation at all.

"Life works in mysterious ways," she murmured. "Your sister's death led you to prevent many more."

She glanced up at him, looked pensive. "Don't take this the wrong way, because I truly am sorry about your sister, but I'm glad you're a pediatric heart surgeon. Very glad."

Ryder nodded. "It's all I've ever wanted to be."

"It's what you were meant to be."

Maybe. He'd never considered any other profession, not even as a small child when friends would say firefighter, police officer, or professional athlete. Ryder had surprised people by saying he was going to be a pediatric cardiothoracic surgeon.

And that's what he'd done.

For Chrissy.

For his parents.

For himself.

A warm hand wrapped around his and gave a gentle squeeze.

Ryder's gaze jerked to McKenzie's green one and what he saw there had him feeling as if the elevator cable had snapped and they were spiraling downward.

Fortunately, he was saved by the elevator coming to a stop and the door sliding open.

He immediately pulled his hand from McKenzie's, resisted the urge to shake away the electricity still zinging up and down his arm.

He needed to be careful.

It would be way too easy to forget she was on the rebound of a broken heart.

CHAPTER FOUR

AN EXHAUSTED RYDER leaned back against the wall in the small doctors' lounge nestled between the men and women's locker rooms. He'd showered, put fresh scrubs on post having been in the operating room with McKenzie and the rest of the multifaceted team that had worked to repair Sawyer's heart over the last seven hours.

He'd been in the operating room for greater than twelve hours on the same procedure in the past when unfortunate complications had arisen, such as bleeding or discovering more anomalies than expected. But typically, an uncomplicated Norwood operation took him around five hours.

Sawyer's had been uncomplicated other than difficulty weaning her off the heart/lung bypass machine. It had taken an extra couple of hours for her little heart to start beating efficiently on its own, but it finally had.

"You okay?"

Ryder's gaze lifted and met McKenzie's green one. Had she come to the lounge looking for him?

He straightened, ran his hand through his hair, then shrugged. "Norwoods are my least favorite surgery to do."

"You and the rest of the team did a great job," she praised, her eyes darkening. "I worried when Sawyer didn't initially respond to being weaned off the life support. I thought we were all going to break out clapping when she finally did."

He'd certainly been clapping in his head. Clapping, jumping for joy, high-fiving his teammates. Sawyer getting off that heart/lung bypass machine as quickly as possible was important.

"You played a huge role in that great job," he reminded her.

Her, the pediatric cardiac anesthesiologist, another pediatric cardiothoracic surgeon, a pediatric intensivist, numerous nurses and surgical technicians—the entire surgical team had done an excellent job.

"Thank you for including me on the team."

Ryder nodded. McKenzie had been on his surgical teams in the past, but she'd never been his first choice of cardiologist. Not that she wasn't excellent at what she did, just that he hadn't wanted the interaction—and his not requesting her in no way hurt her career as Dr. Rhea and another of the pediatric cardiothoracic surgeons preferred her as part of their surgical teams and always requested her first.

Like him, she'd showered and was dressed in fresh scrubs. Her auburn hair was pulled back in a ponytail and a few freckles could be seen across her nose and cheeks. He'd thought it hundreds of times, but McKenzie's ex was a fool.

"You headed home?"

"No, I'm going to check on a few patients, chart, check on Sawyer again, and—" she gave a wry smile "—somewhere during all that, grab something to eat."

"No rest for the wicked," he teased. Teasing her felt good, eased some of the exhaustion cloaking him.

"Speaking of which, you look like you need to crash for a few hours."

He chuckled. Obviously teasing her hadn't eased his fatigue enough. "Is that a nice way of you telling me I look bad?"

Her cheeks reddened. "That's not what I meant. You just appear tired."

"Like I said, Norwoods aren't my favorite."

"Because of the high mortality rate?"

Not surprised she'd immediately guessed his reason, Ryder nodded. "No doctor wants to go into a procedure that only has an eighty-five percent survival rate."

"Your personal percentage is right at ninety."

He wasn't surprised she knew his stats. All the surgeons at the hospital had above-average percentages and the hospital was proud of that fact. Ryder knew the numbers could be better.

"That's still one out of every ten babies who won't make it to their first birthday." Which gutted him, because that one who didn't make it, that one was someone's Chrissy.

"And nine who will because you reconstructed their heart to where it provides their body with oxygenated blood," McKenzie reminded him, her chin lifting as if to say she'd counter everything he said with something positive. "Sawyer is going to be one of those nine. She's a fighter."

"I hope so." He prayed all his patients survived, even when the odds were stacked against them.

"I'd not really planned to sit down to eat, just to get a yogurt or something since I really do need to check on a few patients." She pinned him with her gaze. "If you planned to head that way, maybe we could walk to the cafeteria together?"

Ryder hesitated. He'd been with McKenzie most of the day, would be with her for an entire weekend. What would walking with her to the cafeteria hurt?

"Sure. I'll walk with you."

"I…" She took a deep breath. "I really appreciate you going with me to Tennessee, Ryder. I know how busy you are and truly if you ever need my help with anything, I've got your back."

Was that why she'd sought him out? To thank him again for agreeing to go with her? He probably shouldn't have for his own peace of mind, but still felt it was the honorable thing to do.

"Knowing I don't have to worry about you getting the wrong idea or having unrealistic expectations from the weekend is such a relief," she rushed on. "That's why I had considered going the hired escort route, so I didn't have the messiness of inviting someone who wouldn't understand that I need the relationship to appear real even though I'm not interested in a real relationship."

Which was good for him to keep in mind. He didn't want a relationship with a woman on the rebound. McKenzie didn't want a real relationship with him. Maybe, despite the fact he found her physically attractive, they could be friends after Tennessee rather than his having to ignore her.

He'd like that, he realized.

Because he liked McKenzie.

Which was exactly why they couldn't be friends after they returned from Tennessee.

What had she done? McKenzie wondered for the thousandth time since she and Ryder had boarded the plane.

She must be crazy to think she could pull this off, to convince her family that she and Paul had broken up, but that she was ecstatic about it as she was now happily dating her colleague, Dr. Ryder Andrews.

No. Big. Deal.

A piece of cake.

Smooshed cake, but cake.

She could do this, could interact with her family all weekend, smile lots, pretend Ryder was the man of her dreams, and that she was over-the-moon happy in their relationship, that she had no remnant feelings for Clay or Paul. Although, she was beginning to wonder what it was about her that made men date her for years, then dump her.

Two men she'd devoted years of her life to and both had ultimately moved on. Was she so un-lovable? She hadn't thought so, but if she was the one who kept getting dumped that must mean something.

She'd dated only a few other times. Those had all been short-term relationships and she couldn't recall who had quit talking to whom. Was she batting one hundred per cent dumpage?

Ugh. She should probably do some long, hard thinking on that, figure out what was wrong with her that drove men away. But first things first.

She had to ride in this airplane for nineteen hundred and seventy-four miles from Seattle to Nashville.

Ten million, four hundred and twenty-two thousand, seven-hundred and twenty feet.

Not that she was counting.

Flying terrified her.

They'd not even taken off yet and she was al-ready clamoring to get out of the plane but try-ing not to let Ryder know he'd gotten himself into more than he'd bargained for.

Would he have still gone had he known she'd

probably have multiple panic attacks over flying during their travels?

He'd probably go back to avoiding her the moment they returned to Seattle. Which was sad as she'd really enjoyed the times their paths had crossed the past two weeks.

Taking a deep breath, she told herself she had this, all of this; and in particular, her current situation of being strapped into an airplane seat. She'd flown multiple times in the past and always landed safely, right?

Yes, she'd fought a horrific anxiety monster each time, but she had survived, and she would this flight, too.

Throat tight, she glanced over at where Ryder read something on his phone, hoping that looking at him would distract her from the clawing at her composure.

For now, she'd keep a brave face on and remind herself why she was on the plane.

Yeah, she knew why she was doing this crazy trip to Tennessee.

What she couldn't understand was why Ryder had been willing to adjust his already long hours to work patients in ahead of time so he could easily take off a few days to go with her? Had he needed an excuse to take a break from work that badly?

Right up until they'd boarded the plane, she'd

expected him to tell her he'd changed his mind. Why hadn't he?

Had boredom been his reason for saying yes? Perhaps he felt sorry for his dateless colleague and was making her his charity case for the year? Or maybe he'd once had a wedding to go to during a downtime in his life and could relate to how she felt—dumped, dateless and desperate.

Ha. As if.

The man was the department heartthrob and had probably never had a dating downtime his whole life, much less been dumped and desperate.

"Why are you doing this?"

He glanced up from the phone screen. "Reading an article about two-photon polymerization? Because I'm interested in how this technique is being used to achieve scaffolding in 3D printing of human tissue."

McKenzie blinked. That's what he was reading? Not that she was surprised. If ever there had existed a sexy brainiac, Ryder would fit that bill. The looks of a Greek god. A brain that rivaled the nerdiest nerd. She'd always recognized that he was the ultimate package. Only she'd been happy with Paul and hadn't really ever thought about Ryder as anything more than a colleague who'd gone from friendly to avoidance.

Sitting next to him, she noticed. Just as she'd noticed the women eyeing him while they'd waited to board the plane. They'd all looked at her with envy. Ha. If they only knew.

"Isn't that what you're doing in the lab with the laser?" she asked, hoping he'd talk with her to help distract her from their surroundings.

She didn't know a lot of the intricate details, but exciting things were happening at Trevane Technologies in the field of 3D printing human tissue and Ryder headed the clinical aspect of the research in regard to applying it to congenital cardiac diseases.

"Yes, that's one part of what we're doing in the lab," he admitted, tapping his phone. "The article depicts the research a material science institute is doing and what they've achieved using a similar process to bioprinting. Although what we're doing at Trevane is eons ahead in some aspects, their speeds for laying down tissue far exceed anything we've achieved."

"Faster isn't always better," she mused, glancing out the window, then wishing she hadn't. The last of the luggage had been loaded and they'd soon be preparing for takeoff.

"In this case, faster is better. Keeping the printed cells alive is the biggest challenge facing us on creating usable human tissue. If we can successfully print tissue faster, then hopefully we can achieve thicker layers without deoxygenation. Thicker layers means someday being able to 3Dprint vessels, valves, heart chambers or maybe even entire hearts." Passion filled his words. "Can you imagine the implications if we could make a heart for patients needing a transplant rather than having to wait on a donor?"

The thought was mind-boggling, but something that was becoming more and more of a possibility. The research to further develop valve and heart tissue regeneration via bioprinting normally excited her because of what it meant for her patients, for all cardiac patients, and other disease states, too, as the principles carried far greater potential than just with cardiac care.

But, currently, she fought the sensation of panic's hands gripping her throat and squeezing with all their might.

"I'm familiar with Professor Ovikov's work," he continued now that she'd gotten his attention. "We met years ago when 3Dprinting of live tissue was still in its infancy. Brilliant scientist."

Something in the way he said the praise allowed McKenzie to force her blurring gaze away from the window and her mind not to register that the crew had closed the plane door and were moving about the cabin, checking the overhead bins one last time.

And then, they'd take off.

Talk to Ryder. Just carry on a conversation as if nothing monumental was about to happen.

As if she wasn't about to be flung through the

air at speeds she was positive humans weren't meant to travel.

"Dr. Ovikov probably says the same about you," she managed to get out despite her mouth deciding to imitate the Sahara. Seriously, how could her tongue be sticking to the roof of her mouth when her palms were sweating like crazy?

Statistics alone said she was safer flying than driving, right? Her brother constantly tossed that out at her when she complained about his chosen career path as a pilot.

"Maybe, but I doubt it," Ryder admitted, staring at her as if he was starting to pick up on the fact that she wasn't her normal calm, cool, collected self.

Ha. If he only knew how far from the dedicated pediatric cardiologist she felt.

"Our research overlaps and we have similar goals," he continued, his honey-colored eyes darkening as he studied her.

Just keep talking. Distraction was the best way through this. They'd soon be in the air. Then she'd settle down a little. She didn't like any part of flying but takeoffs and landings were always the worst. Always.

Ryder probably already regretted agreeing to do this wedding weekend. The last thing she needed was to freak out on him before they were even out of Seattle.

His gaze had narrowed.

Yeah, he was definitely on to her.

She swallowed, fought to keep her tone steady, and forced a smile to her slowly numbing face. "Is that a nice way of saying he's your competition for upcoming grants?"

See, she sounded semi-normal. Her voice had broken only a little.

"She," Ryder corrected, his expression saying he'd caught that tiny vocal glitch. "Dr. Anna Ovikov."

Something in the way he said *she* truly distracted McKenzie from the plane as she wondered just what his relationship had been with said "she."

Professional or something more?

She mentally scolded herself.

Look at her. Getting all curious about a pretend boyfriend.

"That's fine. Go ahead. Read her research. Just don't forget why you're here," she reminded him, digging her fingers into the airplane seat to the point she was surprised her nails didn't break.

"How could I forget," he teased, the corner of his mouth lifting even though his eyes were still dark with concern. "It's not every day I play a coworker's pretend boyfriend."

"Shh," McKenzie scolded, looking around to see if any of the other passengers had heard what he'd said. Across the aisle from him sat a teen-aged boy wearing earbuds with his eyes closed.

His mother was engrossed in a book. Neither was paying the least bit of attention to her and Ryder. "You can't say such things. You never know who's listening. You have to stay in role at all times this weekend."

His brow lifted. "You're sure just telling your family the truth wouldn't be easier?"

"Positive." For so many reasons. "You don't know my mother."

She would be all aflutter trying to make sure McKenzie was really okay with the wedding, would be devastated that McKenzie had been dumped again, especially right before Reva and Jeremy's wedding. She'd feel obligated to do something, anything, to make McKenzie feel better. Which would make her feel only worse. She didn't want her mother setting her up on blind dates or throwing men at her all weekend.

And then, there was Reva.

Beautiful Reva who was always the belle of the ball but had always felt guilty if McKenzie hadn't been included. Reva always included her. Her cousin would have major guilt at her own happiness if McKenzie was suffering from heartbreak.

Everyone would be worried about her, wanting her to move home so they could help nurse her broken heart. They'd never leave her alone.

She'd just have to prove to them that she was happy, didn't need their interference or pity.

Ryder was that proof.

"But I will know your mother soon."

Which almost made her as nervous as the thought of the plane taking off.

"Yes, you will." Swallowing, she dug her fingertips deeper into the seat as she held Ryder's gaze. "Just make sure you act as if you really are my boyfriend. Please. It's important my family believes you're crazy about me."

If they thought her happy, they wouldn't worry. Not worrying meant not meddling.

He didn't look concerned. "Shouldn't be a problem."

The air in the plane was so thin. Any moment she expected her knuckles to break through the clenched skin of her fingers.

"Because you're certifiable for agreeing to this?"

He grinned. "Something like that."

She was struck again by just how handsome he was. Not that she hadn't always known, just she'd categorized him in her mind to where she'd never thought of him as more than just that—a really hot guy she worked with, who made her uncomfortable with his overabundance of pheromones, and who hadn't liked her.

With his going above and beyond this weekend, with how his smile made things better, she'd never be able to relegate him to two-dimensional again.

He should smile more right now. She needed him to make things better.

She forced herself to take a deep breath, then another. "Truly, I appreciate you doing this."

Even if he'd come only as an excuse to look up an old girlfriend.

"I expect you to return the favor someday."

"By going to a wedding with you as your pretend girlfriend?" Odds were he'd never need her to do any such thing and they both knew it.

"Something like that."

"We've been cleared for takeoff," the captain said over the intercom speaker.

"Oh!" McKenzie gasped and grabbed hold of Ryder's arm. Talking with him, she'd kept that they'd taxied away from the hangar and out onto the airstrip at bay.

They were literally preparing for takeoff.

As in about to leave the ground and zoom through the air as if gravity wasn't a thing to be concerned about.

McKenzie worried about gravity. A lot.

"You okay?"

"Do I look okay?" she bit out, knowing her fingers were digging into his arm but not able to pry them loose. Something about holding onto him made her feel safer.

"Not particularly."

She closed her eyes, knowing any moment the plane was going to start moving again. When it did it wasn't going to slow down for a long, long time.

Five hours. That's all. Just five hours, then she'd be in Nashville and back on the ground.

Help, her mind screamed. Get her off the plane. Pronto. She couldn't do this.

She had to. She'd done it before and landed just fine. She'd do it again. For Reva and the rest of her family.

But, oh, how she wanted to get off the plane.

"McKenzie?"

"Mmm?" she managed, wondering just how thick her throat had swelled because getting air in and out was impossible.

Why couldn't she have just told them all that she couldn't get off work? She hadn't really had to go to Reva's wedding? Her cousin could have gotten a different bridesmaid, could have had her big day without having McKenzie there.

"Open your eyes."

Her mind registered that Ryder had leaned closer, but she didn't do as he'd ordered. Ordered because that's what his words had been, a command.

"McKenzie." His tone was softer, coaxing even, this time. "Open your eyes."

She did so, meeting his gaze, and forcing herself not to look away.

"You're afraid of flying?"

"What gave you that idea?" she ground out between clenched teeth.

He grinned, then surprised her by prying her fingers from their death grip on his arm and lacing their hands. "You forgot to tell me you were afraid of flying."

She hadn't forgotten. She'd just hoped she'd be able to hide her fear. She hadn't flown in over two years and had hoped her phobia wouldn't rear its ugly head to the point she wouldn't be able to control it. Wasn't that what the tablet she'd taken was supposed to help with?

"Too bad I didn't forget to make my flight."

Ryder had the audacity to laugh. "Now, now. You wouldn't want to miss your cousin's wedding."

"Fifty percent of marriages end in divorce," she spouted, thinking her hand would soon be so clammy it would slip right out of his hold. "I should just take my chances that this won't last, and she'll think me brilliant for not wasting my time."

"Such a cynic," Ryder mused, studying her so intently that for a moment his looking at her rivaled her aviophobia.

"A realist." The plane started moving, building momentum as it sped down the runway. Unfortunately, McKenzie's stomach stayed behind. "Oh, God."

"Praying is good."

If McKenzie wasn't sure she was about to die, she'd scold Ryder for making fun of her.

Only her heart was beating as if it thought it had to power the engine to lift the plane off the ground and was doing its best to meet the burgeoning demand.

Five hours.

Five hours she'd be stuck inside this plane thirty or so thousand feet in the air, defying gravity.

Hopefully defying gravity.

She sucked in a breath.

Or more like she tried to suck in a breath, but nothing happened. No air filled her lungs. Just more and more panic taking over as her stomach was lost somewhere on the airstrip.

She couldn't breathe, felt increasing light-headedness.

She was going to die from lack of oxygen on a 747 Jumbo Jet.

Her mind started going hazy as her lungs refused to adjust to accommodate her body's need for oxygen.

"Help," she squeaked out, trying to convey to Ryder that she was a goner.

Not sure what he could do, what anyone could do at this point as they barreled down the runway, she let go of his hand and went for her seatbelt, thinking maybe if she loosened it from where it constricted around her waist, she'd be able to get in a breath.

It didn't make sense that the strap at her waist prevented air from entering her lungs, but she fumbled with the latch, planning to free herself, and do who knew what?

Ryder's hand covered hers before she could work the latch loose.

Still, her insides shook as panic threatened to implode within her.

She couldn't do this.

McKenzie lifted her gaze, planning to tell him as much.

She stared straight into honey-brown eyes that were close, closer than they'd ever been, and they stared back.

Eyes that momentarily stole her breath even further, sparking a new plethora of emotions deep inside her.

They searched hers, seeing everything within her, she was sure, knowing she was wondering what it would feel like to lose herself in those eyes while kissing him.

His lips were even closer. As close as they could possibly be as they covered her own in a kiss.

She should pull back.

She should slap him or do something, right?

Wasn't she supposed to be clamoring for freedom from the plane? For oxygen?

Only oxygen didn't seem so important with Ryder's mouth covering hers, coaxing her to return his kiss as his gaze stayed locked with hers.

She hadn't planned to kiss him, but her lips were doing just that. How could they not when he was so irresistible?

Good grief. She was kissing her pretend boyfriend.

Who she'd thought didn't like her.

He must, though. Otherwise, he wouldn't have agreed to this crazy wedding trip.

Or be kissing her, right?

Whether she wanted to give a response or not, his lips were firm against hers, delighted by her reaction.

McKenzie reacted. Oh, how her insides were reacting to Ryder's mouth on hers.

If she'd ever wondered, which she hadn't, not even in her wildest dreams, now she knew.

Dr. Ryder Andrews was excellent at mouth-to-mouth resuscitation.

CHAPTER FIVE

RYDER HAD WITNESSED only a few panic attacks during his lifetime, but he'd seen the alarm in McKenzie's eyes moments before they'd squeezed shut, had watched her frantic movements, and knew he had to do something to defuse the situation.

He hadn't planned on kissing her.

He'd meant to take her hand into his and offer reassurance. Instead, when her lips had started moving toward him, he'd instinctively pressed his lips to them.

Bold, perhaps wrong, but the terror on her face had disappeared almost instantly, replaced with surprise. Any moment he expected a new wave of panic to fill her eyes when she registered that they were kissing.

Panic was filling him that they were kissing.

Because his automatic reaction of wanting to soothe her, to stop her anxiety, might destroy everything.

Fortunately, the fear didn't return in those gorgeous green eyes.

Instead, her gaze darkened with curiosity. Soft, pliable lips willingly met his.

Which might explain the mounting panic in his own gut.

What was he doing kissing McKenzie?

She was using him for the weekend. He knew upfront that he was nothing more than a means to an end.

Kissing her before they'd taken off the ground might not have been his smoothest move.

Because she was kissing him back and that edgy sensation in his stomach wasn't because the plane had lifted off and was ascending at a rapid rate.

He was miles high in ways that had nothing to do with leaving the ground.

He and McKenzie were kissing.

Holding her gaze, his grip on her hand eased, cupping her face instead as he explored the recesses of her pliant mouth, thrilling as she continued to kiss him.

When he pulled away, he stared into her hazy eyes, and waited to see what she'd say. Would she think he'd taken advantage of her near panic attack?

She inhaled a deep breath and stunned him by saying, "Someone should market that."

Not even close to what he'd expected her to say about their kiss.

She took a quick glance out the window, then nervously back toward him. "I didn't even notice when the plane lifted off the ground. That's amazing. Thank you so much!"

"You're welcome?" Ryder blinked, not quite sure how to take her gratitude. McKenzie kissing him back had sucker punched him, leaving his head in the same state she'd been in as the plane had started taxiing—a panicked mess.

Kissing her was dangerous when he had no intention of having a real relationship with her.

She still looked a little addled, but not as she'd been before.

"But I'm not sure how that particular technique could be marketed without a whole lot of backlash."

She took a few deep breaths, but her color remained good. "You're probably right, but I still say you should go for it."

Which is what he'd done. Gone for it and kissed McKenzie.

"Sorry," he said and meant it. "I shouldn't have done that."

"Are you kidding me?" Her brows veed and she waved away his apology as if the kiss had been no big deal. "You saved me from succumbing to the panic behemoth that grips me at takeoff. Yet something else I owe you for, which I don't like, but thank you for saving me on this, too."

She acted as if the kiss hadn't meant anything.

Ryder wasn't sure if he was grateful or offended that she'd dismissed their kiss so readily.

Offended.

Definitely offended.

His insides were shattered at the electricity their kiss had sparked to life, and she was being flippant about their kiss.

Which was good as he shouldn't have kissed a woman who was vulnerable over having just gotten out of a long-term relationship. You'd think his having mentioned Anna would have been enough to have had him keeping his mouth to himself.

"Now, can you do that for the next five hours until we land?"

Ryder blinked. He couldn't have heard McKenzie correctly.

Before he could respond, she laughed. "I'm kidding, of course, and am mostly just rambling on to distract myself from the fact that we're in the air. I detest flying."

Under different circumstances, Ryder wouldn't have minded kissing her for the next five hours. Circumstances that didn't involve him being the rebound guy.

McKenzie might need a distraction from her fear of flying, but he needed a distraction from their kiss. He'd ponder at how well they fit together and what he was going to do about it later, when he wasn't sitting beside her, when the sweet taste of her lips didn't linger, when she wasn't looking at him as if she really did want him to kiss her again.

She settled back into her seat, closed her eyes, and took several deep, measured breaths that told him she wasn't as over her anxiety as she let on.

Either that, or his kiss had shaken her more than she'd said. His guess was on the flight being the cause, though.

"Have you always been afraid to fly, McKenzie?"

She grimaced and didn't open her eyes as she said, "Since I was six."

Six. That was specific, but it wasn't so much her words as how the color had drained from her face that had him curious.

"What happened when you were six?"

Would Ryder understand if McKenzie said she didn't want to talk about the reasons why she hated flying?

Because she never, ever, ever talked about why.

Which made her next words surprise her as much as they must have him.

"My dad died in a plane crash."

Eyes squeezed tightly shut, she felt Ryder's movement in the seat next to her, wasn't surprised when his hand covered hers again. Strong, warm, talented hands that repaired his patients' hearts.

If only he could repair all the broken things about hers.

"I'm sorry, McKenzie."

"Me, too," she whispered, keeping her eyes closed as if that could somehow block out that she'd told him what she'd never told Paul.

Why was that?

She'd planned to marry Paul. Ryder was just a colleague who was pretending to be her boyfriend for a weekend wedding. No. Big. Deal.

Only his kiss had been a big deal.

Sure, the flip-flops her belly had done were likely the result of the plane lifting off the ground and nothing to do with his kiss. But Ryder had done what she'd have argued was impossible. He'd distracted her through takeoff.

She might make him a permanent travel accessory.

"What happened?"

She let out a slow breath, trying to push some of her sorrow out along with the air. His was a natural question, just not one she wanted to answer at any time, much less while ascending to thirty thousand feet.

"I suppose now is the worst possible time for me to ask, eh?" He made a noise that was somewhere between a sigh and a groan. "I really am sorry, McKenzie."

"It was a long time ago." Although that day, the aftermath, was heavily imprinted upon her mind to where she could relive the tragedy daily in vivid detail if she'd allow herself to. She didn't.

She certainly wouldn't allow the memories to take hold while on a plane.

"He was a pilot." Hello! Where had that admission come from? What was she doing? She did not want to talk about this.

Opening her eyes, she glanced toward Ryder, saw the empathy and interest in his gaze, and heard herself tell him things she didn't normally say out loud.

Normally?

She never said them out loud.

Never. Ever. Ever. Not to anyone.

"Dad owned a small plane and gave flight lessons." Once upon a time she'd loved to fly. She'd been too young to know any better. "He thought he was invincible." She paused, swallowed the lump in her throat. "He wasn't."

Ryder's thumb brushed over her hand in a soothing caress. "You were six?"

More aware of his touch than she should be, especially given their conversation, she nodded. "My brother was ten."

Ryder's brow lifted. "You have a brother?"

Despite the waterworks threatening to spill from her eyes, she laughed at the surprise in Ryder's voice. "When I claim him."

"You've never mentioned a brother."

"There are a lot of things I've never mentioned to you," she reminded him. "We're work colleagues. Why would I tell you about my personal life?"

Ryder's silence felt heavy between them.

"That may have been true in the past," he finally said. "But now I'm your pretend boyfriend so you should spend the next five hours filling me in on what I need to know for us to pull this off."

"I've been thinking about that," she admitted, her mind racing through all the things she'd dwelled on since he'd agreed to go with her to Tennessee. "We should stick to the truth."

"You've changed your mind about our pretending to date each other?"

Was that excitement she saw on his face? Maybe he really did regret the fiasco he found himself in.

"No, not about that," she shook her head, "although I understand if you want out."

"I don't want out," he assured her. "This is way more interesting than my previous weekend plans."

Which made her wonder just what his weekend plans had been? What had he been willing to give up so that he could go with her to a wedding celebrating people he'd never heard of until a few days ago?

"Good." She sighed her relief. "My family knew I was dating Paul, that he and I had been together for years. They expected us to eventually marry." They could still marry if they got a second chance. "They'll be shocked we broke up." McKenzie was shocked they'd broken up. "They won't question that you and I are a recent development. As such, we won't be expected to know everything about each other."

"True, but there are some things, as a couple, that we should know," he pointed out.

Curious, she asked, "Such as?"

"What's your favorite color?"

"Blue," she answered without hesitation, frowning at him. "Boring question."

He ignored her jab. "Why blue?"

"Because it's the color of the sky."

"This coming from a girl who's afraid to fly."

"Woman," she corrected. "Woman who is afraid to fly. There's no shame in my fear. Lots of people prefer keeping their feet on the ground and I have a good reason for my dislike."

"Agreed." After a moment, he added, "Green."

She cut her gaze toward him.

"Because it's the color of new beginnings."

As in this weekend? she wondered, then frowned at her thought. This wasn't a new beginning.

"And because it's the color of your eyes."

The color of her... McKenzie's breath caught, and her stomach clenched much as it had when he'd kissed her.

Pulling her hand from his, she frowned. "You don't need to lay it on so thick. I'd prefer believable to syrupy sweet with saccharine drizzled on top."

"Nothing thick about saying I like the color of your eyes when I do like the color of your eyes." He settled back into his seat and pulled up the article he'd been engrossed in earlier.

She stared at him, not quite sure what to think, especially when he added, "You have great eyes, McKenzie."

McKenzie swiped at something tickling her nose. As she did so, noises penetrated the hazy world of sleep she dwelt in, stirring her to wakefulness.

She opened her eyes, realized she was pressed up against Ryder's strong shoulder, and that there was a drool spot on his shirt.

Her drool.

Yikes.

She sat up, pretended a poise she didn't possess as she got her bearings and wiped her mouth.

She was sitting next to Ryder in a plane speeding toward Nashville.

Only there were no clouds out the window.

Just lights and other planes breaking up the darkness.

They'd landed!

She glanced at the time on her fitness watch. Good grief. She'd slept through most of the flight and the landing.

How had that happened?

She was glad she'd slept through it.

Only she winced at the tiny damp spot on Ryder's sleeve.

Realizing he was watching her, she grimaced. "Please tell me I didn't snore."

One corner of his mouth lifted. "Only a little."

She couldn't tell if he was teasing or if she truly had. She didn't suppose it mattered with a pretend boyfriend.

It wasn't as if she was trying to impress him.

Only he was a coworker, quite gorgeous, and thought she had great eyes, so it wasn't wrong to want to not totally embarrass herself.

She couldn't believe she'd fallen asleep.

Then again, she'd not slept well since prior to her breakup with Paul. Still, never would she have dreamed she could sleep on a plane.

She gave Ryder a look of gratitude. "Thank you."

"For?"

"Making that the best flight I've ever been on."

Having Ryder beside her had to be how she'd relaxed enough to doze off. Which was odd since he didn't relax her. Far from it.

She'd never felt so far out of her comfort zone as when he'd kissed her. Only...

"By boring you to sleep?" His tone was teasing.

"By helping me unwind enough that I could sleep. Big difference."

Seeming to like her answer, he nodded. "You do look calmer."

Wondering if that was his subtle way of telling her that her makeup was mussed and her hair wild, she stretched to pull her bag out from beneath the seat in front of her.

When she'd retrieved her compact, she glanced in the tiny mirror.

Rather than the mess she expected, her mascara had miraculously stayed on her lashes and wasn't all down her cheeks other than faint smudges she quickly wiped away.

Digging in her bag, she found a lipstick tube.

"No need for that," Ryder assured her, watching her. "You look beautiful."

"Thanks." His compliment warmed her insides, but she put her lipstick on anyway. She'd need all the armor she could muster prior to facing her mother and the rest of the crew.

Too bad lipstick didn't come in chainmail.

Who'd have thought Ryder's calm, cool and collected pediatric cardiologist colleague was terrified to fly, albeit, she certainly had good reason?

Or that she'd be nervous as a kitten about seeing her family?

Or maybe it was her family meeting him that had her so on edge?

"Is someone meeting us?"

She shook her head. "My brother offered, but

I wanted us to have our own transportation. I arranged for a rental car."

"In case we need to make a quick escape?" he teased, hoping to elicit a smile, even if just a small one.

She didn't, just nodded. "Exactly."

Which made him wonder about McKenzie's relationship with her family. She'd considered hiring an escort service to keep from making the trip home alone. Just what kind of pressure had her family put on her in the past?

"Surely they aren't that bad?"

Shaking her head, McKenzie sighed. "They're not bad, just think it's within their right to meddle in my life. Always have and likely always will try to."

"Is that why you moved across the country? To get away from them?"

"Of course not." But she hesitated long enough that he wasn't sure she bought her answer any more than he did. "But my mother did once sign me up for a speed round dating service night. And then there was the time she contacted local churches to find out if they had programs for singles to meet."

"Seriously?"

McKenzie nodded. "Oh, yeah. Mama has no problem with meddling in my life even from half the country away."

"Is that why you ended up in Seattle?" he wondered out loud.

"I visited Seattle with a group of friends while in med school and fell in love with Pike Place Market and just everything about the city." Her appreciation for the city sparked to life in her eyes. "I applied for residency there, got it, fell further in love with the city, and when I was offered a permanent position at Seattle Cardiac Clinic for Kids, I stayed. How about you?"

"Similar story in some ways. I'm originally from Atlanta, went to medical school in Birmingham, did a cardiology, then a surgery residency in Pittsburgh, then took the positions with Trevane and Seattle Cardiac Clinic for Kids."

Ryder stood, stretched out his six-foot-plus frame as best as he could in the plane aisle, before grabbing their carry-on bags from the overhead bin.

She stood, double-checked their seats to make sure they hadn't left anything, then took her bag from him. "Thanks."

Once inside Nashville Airport, they made a pit stop, then went to the lower level where McKenzie had made arrangements to pick up a rental car.

"Nice," Ryder teased when the clerk handed over the keys to a minivan.

"This isn't what I purchased," McKenzie argued, but to no avail.

Ryder didn't mind, but McKenzie had the clerk

checking again to make sure there wasn't another option.

He'd stowed their bags in the back of the minivan.

"I'm driving since I know where I'm going," she informed him, climbing into the driver's seat.

They made a quick late-night fast-food run, but otherwise it was only a twenty-minute drive from the airport. The closer they got to McKenzie's family's house, the tenser she got.

The house was a moderate-size old-style ranch.

"Be prepared for anything," McKenzie warned as they got their luggage out of the van. "It wouldn't surprise me if they were all here and jumped out at us when we walk in. Aunt Myrtle may or may not be dressed if that happens."

Ryder's curiosity was piqued, but the only person who'd waited on them was McKenzie's mother. They'd not made it up to the porch when the front door flung open and the petite woman hurried out to wrap her arms around McKenzie.

"Hello, Mama," McKenzie whispered just loud enough he could hear. "I've missed you, too."

"Let me look at you," her mother exclaimed, pulling back and eyeing McKenzie in the porch light.

"Don't you dare comment on how I've grown," McKenzie warned, but was smiling and glassy-eyed.

Ryder could see that despite the fact McKenzie

thoughts had gone. "No worries. I'm so glad you're home."

"Me, too," she said and meant it. It had been too long since she'd been home, but Seattle was a long way from Nashville for someone terrified of flying. It wasn't as if she could just hop in her car and go home for a quick visit.

But she could have come home for a visit, a voice nagged. Could have and should have.

Maybe, just maybe her flight back to Seattle would be as smooth as the flight to Nashville and she could put to rest some of her flying fears. Doubtful, but the flight there hadn't been nearly as bad as expected. Thanks to Ryder.

Her mother gave him a sly look. "And don't even think you're sleeping on my sofa, young man. I won't have it."

McKenzie shrugged. "I'll take the sofa."

Both her mother and Ryder launched into arguments of why that wasn't happening. Fatigue washed over her. It really had been a long day and she was exhausted.

"I told you I'm a modern woman." Her mother pointed Ryder in the direction of McKenzie's old room.

He looked toward her for guidance.

Too tired to care what he thought, she told him, "You may as well follow me."

Once her mother had given them both another round of hugs and closed the door behind her as

lived so far away, there was no shortage of love between the two women.

"Grown? Ha, you look as if I need to put some meat on you. You're nothing but skin and bones," her mother countered, which Ryder found interesting as McKenzie's mother was a tiny thing herself. "This must be your new guy."

"Mama, this is Dr. Ryder Andrews." She gave him a here goes everything look. "Ryder, this is my mother, Roberta Wilkes."

Ryder smiled at the petite woman with dark eyes and hair. Although he could see the resemblance between McKenzie and her mother in bone structure and body build, McKenzie must have gotten her coloring from her father.

He stuck out his hand. "Nice to meet you."

McKenzie's mother clasped his hand between hers, then dropped his hand and gave him the biggest hug he'd ever had. "We are so glad to finally meet you."

McKenzie sighed. "Mom, you make it sound as if I've been hiding him away. Ryder and I haven't been dating that long. Just a few weeks."

Roberta gave her daughter a pert look. "Long enough that you brought him home to Reva's wedding."

"There is that. Sorry, Ryder." She turned to her mother. "It's late, Mama. We have a busy few days ahead of us, and we're worn out. Can you let us know where we're sleeping?"

Their rooms ended up being McKenzie's room. As in singular.

"Your cousin Jeffrey and his wife and kids are in your brother's old room. Your brother won't be in until tomorrow and says he'll take the sofa."

"I can take the sofa," Ryder offered despite knowing his six-foot frame wouldn't comfortably fit. It was the right thing to do and he had to halt the panic rising in McKenzie's eyes.

"That isn't necessary," Roberta assured him, looking quite proud of herself. "I'm a modern woman."

"You were a modern woman before women were modern," McKenzie said under her breath, but Ryder heard.

Perhaps her mother had, too, as she gave McKenzie a stern look before smiling at Ryder. "You'll have to excuse my daughter. Flying addles her mind a little."

CHAPTER SIX

NOT IN A million years had McKenzie ever envisioned that she'd someday be standing in her childhood bedroom with Dr. Ryder Andrews, with him pretending to be her boyfriend.

One just never knew where life was going to take them.

Most women would be arguing to get Ryder into their bedroom. Here McKenzie was trying to figure a way to keep him out and coming up short for a feasible reason that wouldn't raise her family's suspicions.

"Sorry, Mom," she sighed. "I'm exhausted and like I said, we have a big few days. I want to hit the sack if that's okay. It's been a long day and flight."

They both knew how traumatizing boarding the plane and the five-hour flight was for her.

Or that it usually was.

She still couldn't believe she'd fallen asleep on Ryder's shoulder and missed almost the entire flight and all of the landing.

Best. Flight. Ever.

Her mother leaned in and gave another big squeeze, as if she knew where McKenzie's

she left the small bedroom, McKenzie's shoulders sagged. She sank onto the edge of the full-sized bed to stare at the man who hadn't moved from the spot near the door. Was he thinking of making a run for it yet?

She wouldn't blame him.

"I'm sorry."

"For what?"

"That. This." She stretched her arm out to indicate the room where he was trapped sleeping with her. "I'll take the floor and you can have the bed."

"Quit stealing my lines."

"You're doing me a favor. I should be the one to take the floor."

He shook his head. "Not happening."

She gave him a tired smile. "Thank you, Ryder. Just know I appreciate you being here."

His smile filled her with warmth.

"You're welcome, McKenzie. It's been interesting."

No doubt. From her fear of flying to drooling on his shoulder to meeting her mother, he hadn't seemed bored or shown the slightest irritation, just patience and a kindness that surprised her. Although, she wasn't sure why as she'd witnessed the same traits demonstrated with how he treated his patients.

"You want the bathroom first?" she offered, pointing to a door on the opposite side of the room. "It's a Jack and Jill, which means my cousin Jeff, his wife and kids are on the other side so watch the noise. Hopefully, they haven't left it too messy, but check the lid just in case. They have a four-year-old son."

Ryder chuckled. "Brings me back to my college dorm days. You sure you want me to go first?"

She nodded and watched as he grabbed his shaving kit bag from his suitcase, along with pajama bottoms and a T-shirt, before he headed into the bathroom.

Once the door closed, she fell back against her bed and stared at a spot on the ceiling.

Truth was Ryder had been a much better travel companion that she'd expected. Probably better than Paul would have been.

Paul would have complained about her drooling on his trendy clothes and leaving him to entertain himself during the flight.

Ryder had been…nice.

Nice? Calling his kiss nice seemed almost an insult. The man could kiss.

No wonder she'd done just fine during takeoff. His kiss had sent her mind soaring before the plane had ever left the ground.

Which confused her. Less than a month ago she'd hoped to someday marry Paul and spend her life with him. How was it Ryder's kiss had electrified her, left her wanting more?

She shouldn't want Ryder to kiss her. Shouldn't be thinking about his kiss. He'd kissed her only to stop her panic attack. She'd kissed him only because she'd been panicked.

Knowing she was going to pass out if she didn't get out of the bed, she forced herself up and began unpacking her suitcase and storing the items into her closet. She paused to smile at some of the things her mother still had hanging as if they were waiting on McKenzie to come home to wear them after all these years. A jacket with a basketball emblem emblazoned on the sleeve had her reaching out to touch the well-worn material.

Good grief, her prom dress even hung in there. Why would her mother keep that? Even if McKenzie had wanted to wear the dress, she wouldn't be able to shimmy that tiny dress up past her hips, much less zip the thing.

When Ryder had finished in the bathroom and came back into McKenzie's room, she'd finished unpacking her suitcase and was pushing the bag into her closet.

Glancing over to where he walked toward his suitcase, her gaze collided with bare feet.

She gulped.

She'd never been a foot person, quite the opposite, but Ryder's feet were sexy. Her gaze rose higher, taking in his flannel pajama bottoms that somehow managed to look like they belonged in an ad, over his Seattle sport team T-shirt that looked soft, well-worn and accentuated his waist and shoulders.

She should have just stopped right there and looked away, but she didn't. Instead, her eyes moved onward to pause at his lips.

His lips that had kissed her on the plane.

Kissed her quite thoroughly. Her lips tingled at the memory. All of her tingled at the memory.

Tingly pleasure swept over her. Then, realizing she was gawking at him, heat flooded her face.

Get your mind away from that kiss, she ordered herself. Thinking about kissing Ryder when he was in her bedroom was not okay.

None of this was real.

Her gaze caught his honey-colored one.

Oh, yeah, he knew she'd been checking him out. Her face burned. He was here as a favor. What was wrong with her that she was looking at Ryder as if…as if this was real?

He was hot and outdid any teenaged fantasies she'd ever dreamed up in this room. Or anywhere else. Just wow.

And not where her mind should have gone about a pretend boyfriend.

Seeing Ryder at the hospital and clinic and acknowledging that he was drop-dead gorgeous was one thing. Having him in her bedroom and perusing him in a completely sexual way was quite another.

She needed to get her head on straight. No doubt her reaction was just extreme travel weariness and her intense emotions to flying including gratitude for his distraction.

She straightened from where she'd been kneeling, putting the suitcase in her closet, and pasted a smile on her still-flaming face as if she hadn't been looking at him as if he were chocolate dipped and she were a chocoholic ready to binge.

Ryder dropped his toiletries bag on top of his suitcase, then turned toward McKenzie. His lips twitching, he arched a brow. "All unpacked?"

She stood just a few feet away—anywhere in the room was only a few feet away.

"Um, yeah. You're welcome to hang anything you want to in my closet." Her cheeks flushing, she immediately averted her eyes.

McKenzie had never looked at him the way she currently was.

As if she was seeing him as a man. A desirable man.

Okay, maybe during their kiss, but he wasn't sure because she'd been so focused on the plane ride and had acted so no-big-deal afterward.

But in that moment their eyes met, hers had glowed as if she liked what she saw. A lot.

Ryder felt his own cheeks flush, knew he needed to get his thoughts back under control because nothing could happen physically between them.

Not tonight or at any point that weekend.

McKenzie was vulnerable, on the rebound. Ryder refused to be a rebound fling.

"I...um..." She paused, gave him a tentative smile that set warning bells off in his head. "I'm going to brush my teeth and change into my pajamas. Take my bed, please."

Take her bed, please? McKenzie thought, mortified as she washed her face and went through the motions of getting ready to go to sleep.

With Ryder in her bed.

Ryder whom she'd worked with for months and who she'd always agreed with her coworkers was easy on the eyes. But McKenzie had never really seen him. Because Ryder had always made her nervous when he was around, she'd never let herself fully take in just how sexy he was.

Had she known that if she'd let herself, she could have fallen into fantasizing about him, so she'd kept blinders on to avoid a guilty conscience since she'd been committed to Paul?

Ryder was hot.

Scorching.

Glancing at herself in the bathroom mirror one last time, she frowned at the haggardness of her features.

Yeah, Ryder looked fab after hours of travel. She just looked tuckered out.

Fine. Despite her sudden acute awareness of his overabundance of maleness, they weren't really dating. He was her pretend boyfriend and they weren't about to do anything except make a trip to night-night land.

Even if part of her wished this was real, that she and Ryder were embarking on a real relationship, that the sexual tension she felt was more than just her sudden awakening to his overabundance of testosterone.

When she tiptoed back into her room, closing and locking the adjoining bathroom door, she came to a halt.

"You're not in my bed," she accused, frowning at where he'd made a pallet of sorts on the floor with a fuzzy blanket he'd pulled from the foot of her bed. He had one of her old throw pillows tucked beneath his head. It wasn't much of a pallet and there wasn't an extra blanket for him to cover up with unless he took the comforter.

"You take the bed."

"Ryder," she began, feeling guilty that he was at her feet.

"There is no way I'm sleeping in your bed and making you take the floor."

McKenzie eyed where he lay on the floor, then her full-size bed, and came to a quick decision. "Fine. We'll both sleep in the bed."

She'd keep her fantasies and her hands to herself.

His eyes danced. "You must have liked our kiss better than I thought."

Cheeks heating, McKenzie tossed a throw pillow at him. "For that I should leave you on the floor."

Sitting up to catch the pillow, he chuckled. "You definitely should."

Something in the way he said his words, or maybe it was the way he was looking at her, shot a burst of feminine awareness through McKenzie.

"I'm not sure I'd trust myself if I was in that bed with you."

Her breath caught. "You wouldn't hurt me."

She knew he wouldn't. Not even for a second did she believe otherwise.

"Never, but I'm a healthy man with normal sexual urges and you're a beautiful woman." His grin was a bit lopsided, but then his face took on a more serious expression. "Trust me, it's better if I stay on the floor."

McKenzie's heart raced at his words, at what he was saying. If they both slept in the bed he thought they might have sex. She didn't sleep around. But, the way her body was reacting to the thought of having sex with Ryder, she knew he was right.

"It's not as if I wouldn't stop you if you were doing something I didn't want you to be doing." Good grief. She'd practically just told him that she wasn't opposed to their having sex.

Staring at him on the floor, she wondered what it would be like to have sex with Ryder. To kiss him with abandon? To be kissed by him, her lips, her neck, her breasts? To press her body next to his, skin to skin, nothing between them as they moved in pleasure?

Tingles ran up and down her spine. Tingles all over her.

Any moment she was going to throw back the covers and invite him to join her there.

"True, but you're very tempting."

"Are you saying you want me?" How she found the nerve to ask, she wasn't sure, just that the question spilled from her lips. Her gaze remained locked with his as she waited for his answer.

Looking way too sexy for a man sitting on a makeshift bed on the floor, he hesitated only a moment. "I'm not saying I don't. But I won't have sex with you this weekend, McKenzie. You're just out of a long relationship, this is pretend and neither of us want it to be real."

He's wrong, she thought. She did want it to be real. Real enough that he climbed into her bed and... McKenzie's cheeks heated.

Or maybe it was the visions that danced through her head at his "normal sexual urges."

Goodness, he must give off some major pheromones because she so didn't think like this. This looking at a man and wanting him to give in to his "normal sexual urges" and touch her.

Especially a man she barely knew.

And worked with.

And who always made her jumpy.

Maybe because he was a sexy beast and she just hadn't added up that it was the sexual vibes he gave off that made her uneasy. Sex was good, but not something she'd ever dwelt upon.

The heat in Ryder's eyes said he didn't feel the same.

Sex mattered in Ryder's world.

Looking at him, sex mattered in McKenzie's world, too.

Realizing he was probably giving up a highly sexed weekend to accompany her, McKenzie made a mental note to buy him a bottle of his favorite wine when they got back to Seattle.

Because as flustered as he had her hormones and mind, he was right. They shouldn't have sex.

But she wanted to.

And that knowledge blew her mind.

Trying to clear her head, she stared at him, wondering how she could have ever been around him and not registered how charming his grin was.

"You're right. Neither of us want a real relationship and won't be having sex this weekend." She climbed into her bed, pulled the comforter free, and tossed it on the floor, leaving only the sheet to cover herself. With as heated as she currently felt, that should be plenty. "Now you have something to cuddle with."

From the floor, he chuckled, the sound of

which continued to warm her insides all toasty in ways she really didn't like. Pretend boyfriends were not supposed to make their pretend girl-friends feel toasty.

"Night, McKenzie."

Lying in her bed from her teenaged years with Ryder lying on her floor seemed surreal, but no more so than the fact he'd kissed her on the plane. Or that she'd looked at him and had a visual flash of having sex with him.

"Goodnight," she whispered, closing her eyes and thinking her mind might be racing too much to sleep.

And that if sleep did come, she prayed it wouldn't be filled with dreams of the man on the floor next to her bed.

"Sweet dreams."

"Stop that," she ordered without opening her eyes.

"What?" he asked, all innocent, as if he hadn't just read her thoughts again.

"Talking when I'm trying to sleep."

He laughed and McKenzie's mouth curved up-ward as sleep took hold with the sweetest dreams filling her mind.

Someone was in the shower, singing.

The thought hit McKenzie as she rolled over in bed and let her arm flop over the side.

When her hand came into contact with warm

flesh, her eyes flew open at the same time as she jerked her hand away.

Where she was, who she was with, whose warm flesh that had been, registered instantly.

"Good morning to you, too." The man she'd just hit chuckled from the floor.

Glancing at Ryder over the edge of the bed, she wrinkled her nose. "Morning."

"Sounds as if someone's having a good morning," he mused, stretching his arms up over his head, pulling his T-shirt tight over his chest and abs.

McKenzie squeezed her eyes shut and fell back against her bed. This was a new day and she wasn't letting her mind go to where it had been as she'd drifted off to sleep.

Ha. She was pretty sure her mind had been in an orgasmic sexual dreamworld with Ryder all night.

"Sounds like my cousin Jeff." If anything could get her mind off sex it was thoughts of her cousin Jeff.

"You have a big family?"

"Big enough." Which really wasn't much of an answer, she realized. "My dad and mother both had a sister apiece, so I've a few cousins and extended family. Most live around here, but a few of us have escaped."

"You seemed happy to see your mother."

"I was. I am," she corrected. "It's been a long

time since I've been home. I guess you figured that out last night."

"Because you don't like flying?"

"Among other things."

"I want to ask…"

"But you're not going to because you know I'm not going to answer," she cut in, sitting up on the side of the bed. "Is it really morning? Because I just want to sleep a few more hours."

"Makes sense since we're in a different time zone."

"Quit being all logical."

"Fine." He grinned. "I'll be illogical."

"Ha. I think you covered that when you agreed to come with me this weekend."

He shrugged. "It's not been bad so far."

"Besides the near panic attack and having to sleep on the floor," she teased, appreciating his comment that it hadn't been bad more than she should.

"Besides those things," he agreed, still grinning as he let his gaze run over her.

Self-conscious of her first-thing-in-the-morning appearance when he looked so amazing with his sleep-tousled hair and quick smile, McKenzie frowned. "What?"

"Just taking in the real McKenzie."

"As opposed to the fake McKenzie you normally see?" Normally he didn't spend much time looking at her, period.

"Not fake," he said with way more consideration than the early morning warranted. "Just always well put together."

She half-smiled at her current state of morning hair, no makeup, and morning-after-travel eyes. "Ha. That's definitely not how anyone would describe me this morning."

"If you're fishing for a compliment, I'll take the bait. You're beautiful."

She hadn't been, but his compliment pleased her.

"Thank you." And then she didn't know what to say as the silence stretched between them, so she got out of bed. "It's possible Jeff will use all the hot water while he gives his full rendition of the greatest eighties," she warned. "I'm going to make some coffee. You want a cup?"

He shook his head. "Never touch the stuff."

Halfway to the door, McKenzie paused to look at him in horror. "Say what?"

He laughed. "That stuff you guzzle by the gallon," he wrinkled his nose, "I never drink it."

He'd noticed she drank coffee?

"I knew there had to be something wrong with you," she mused.

His lips twitched. "If my distaste of coffee is the worst thing you discover about me this weekend then we did good."

"Are there worse things to discover than not liking coffee? Is that even possible?"

He shrugged. "That depends on how much you like coffee."

"Let's just say it flows freely through my veins."

From the bathroom, they heard the connecting door to the other bedroom open and close.

"He's out! I'm headed in there before someone else does!" And with that she scooped up her shower bag and the clothes she'd set out the night before and disappeared into the bathroom.

Ryder stared at the cup of coffee Roberta had put in front of him and wondered if he'd have to down the stuff to keep from offending her. He really didn't like coffee, but apparently McKenzie's family drank it like their lives depended on it.

"So, tell me about your relationship with my daughter."

Roberta clearly wasn't one to waste time. She leaned back in the chair next to his and sipped on her coffee.

"I imagine it's much as McKenzie has told you. We work together, have been seeing each other a few weeks, and she invited me to come with her this weekend."

"She's never brought anyone home before," Roberta pointed out.

"I wouldn't read too much into that as she told me it has been several years since she's been able to come home."

Roberta snorted. "Since she's chosen to come home."

"Flying with her, I'd say it's more than a choice that's kept her away. She told me about her father," he defended. Although he didn't fully understand McKenzie's reasons for staying away, he suspected her fear of flying topped the list.

Roberta looked surprised. "She told you about Phillip?"

Nodding, Ryder picked up the coffee to have something to do with his hands while facing her scrutiny.

"I can't believe she told you about Phillip," she continued. "She never talks about her father. I sent her to several therapists and she still wouldn't talk about what had happened. Why did she tell you?"

Probably because she'd been on the verge of hyperventilating and he'd been in the next seat over.

"Mom, stop grilling Ryder."

"Afraid he can't take it?" a slightly balding man asked as he came into the room, two kids on his heels.

"Jeff!" McKenzie threw her arms around the man who picked her up and spun her around.

When he put her down, McKenzie was laughing.

"Good to see you, cuz. 'Bout time you came to your senses and came home."

"Just for the weekend. No way am I staying long enough for you to be a pain in my butt the way you were most of my life."

"Nothing you didn't deserve," he assured her. "Nashville has babies with bad hearts, too, you know?"

"I know." Her voice was low and held a sad tone when she answered, but then she stooped down to the little girl literally hanging onto her cousin's leg. "Speaking of babies, you sure have grown since I saw you last," she told the child who just stared at her with big eyes. "How old are you now? Twenty?"

Grinning a bit shyly, the girl shook her head and held up three fingers.

"Three?" McKenzie looked impressed. "That's getting big way too fast, if you ask me."

The little boy who was a spitting image of his father only with a thick shock of blond hair stepped forward and held up a handful of fingers. "I'm four."

"Closest thing I've got to grandchildren," Roberta complained in a half whisper meant to be heard by all. "I don't think this girl here is ever going to give me a grandchild of my own. Although," her mother's gaze ran up and down Ryder, "I may be closer than I'd thought to some beautiful grandbabies."

Her face going pink, McKenzie shook her head. "I've no rush to procreate. Besides, I'm sure that brother of mine is giving his best efforts to produce a grandchild."

"If you ask me, he should forget marriage and keep playing the field as long as he can," Jeff interjected, giving Ryder a nudge on the shoulder. "Right, buddy?"

Ryder was one hundred percent sure he'd been led down a rabbit hole where there were no safe answers. The women eyeing him warned he'd best not agree, and his man card was in serious jeopardy with McKenzie's cousin if he didn't at least make a manly grunt.

McKenzie rescued him by noticing what he was holding. "Hey! I thought you said you didn't like coffee."

Everyone in the room glanced at his still-full cup.

"I don't," he admitted. "But I've never had Tennessee coffee, so who knows?"

McKenzie's mother's house was apparently the wedding meeting place headquarters. Ryder was introduced to family members of various ages.

"He's a hunk," Julianna, her cousin Jeff's wife, told McKenzie in a whisper not meant to be overheard, but that Ryder had. "No wonder you preferred him over the computer guy."

"There was nothing wrong with Paul," McKenzie defended, obviously not wanting her family to think poorly of the man she'd spent two years in a relationship with.

"Then why isn't he here with you?"

"Things just…" She glanced toward Ryder, saw he was watching her with interest, then blushing, looked back toward her friend. "We just didn't work out."

"And now you're dating a hottie coworker and brought him to Tennessee to meet your family?"

"That sums it up," McKenzie agreed with a smile Ryder could tell was fake. "I'm dating my hottie coworker and brought him home to meet all of you. Whatever was I thinking?"

Julianna laughed, then shot another glance toward Ryder who pretended as if he had no clue what they were discussing.

"Well, if you ask me," she said, waggling her brows, "this one's a keeper."

"Maybe." McKenzie sent another apologetic look toward Ryder. "It's too early in our relationship to be having this conversation as we've just begun to date, right, Ryder?"

"Oh, I don't know," he teased, not paying heed to her look of warning. "I've always believed that when you meet the right person time doesn't really matter so much."

Several gazes zeroed in on him. "Is McKenzie the right person?"

There was a chemistry between them he'd immediately felt, but she wasn't the woman for him.

He knew better. But he'd promised to impress her family with pretending to be crazy about her, so pretend he would.

"Only thing I can find wrong with her is her predilection for coffee more than me, but other than that, she feels right."

CHAPTER SEVEN

"SORRY ABOUT THAT," McKenzie apologized the moment she was alone with Ryder. Awkward didn't begin to cover how she'd felt about her family putting him on the spot, or herself for that matter. "My family can't fathom that I'm happy without being married."

Not that she didn't want to marry someday, but she really was happy.

"I take it your brother is still single, too?"

"Not for lack of trying. He's been married twice. His job is hard on relationships."

"I still can't believe he's a pilot."

She nodded. "I can't stand the thought of him going up in those planes, but he loves it. As much as Dad did or maybe even more. Mama doesn't say much, but it has to bother her, too."

"But not as much as it bothers you?"

"Why do you say that?"

"Because that's why you don't live here. Because you can't stand knowing when he's in the air."

McKenzie didn't answer. She hadn't really thought about Mark's flying playing into her reasons for not living in Nashville.

"I shouldn't have said that." Ryder reached for her hand and gave a gentle squeeze. "What do I know? I've not even met your brother."

"You're right. You haven't." But he'd seen through her better than she'd seen through herself, because she acknowledged that he was partially right. She hadn't liked being home and knowing when Mark was in the air. Her brother swore he only felt alive in the air. McKenzie felt terrified at just the thought.

But foremost, medicine had led her to Seattle. Clay had just dumped her to head to Boston. She hadn't wanted to stay in Nashville, had seen the residency in Seattle as an opportunity to discover who she was.

She'd met Paul and been dumped again.

She pulled her hand free and walked across the room, stared at the random items on her dresser top prior to turning back to face Ryder.

"His first wife swore if he'd loved her half as much as he'd loved flying they wouldn't have fallen apart."

"Interesting at how you both dealt with your father's death so differently."

"Isn't it, though? Mark was older, had more time flying with Dad. Whereas I had nightmares for years where I was in that plane with him when it crashed." Sweat prickled her skin at the memory. Forcing it away, she sighed. "Look, I hate to abandon you to a few hours of hanging out with

Jeff and his kids, but we ladies are supposed to meet the others at the bridal shop this morning to pick up my dress. Let's hope it fits."

His gaze skimmed over her figure. "Here's hoping. You sure you don't want me to go with you?"

"To a bridal shop?"

"Might be better hanging with you than whatever I'll end up doing with Jeff."

"Possibly." There was no telling what Reva's older brother would have Ryder doing. "I really do appreciate you coming with me this weekend."

"No problem." Ryder watched McKenzie reach for her purse off the dresser. "And, McKenzie?"

She turned toward him.

"I'm sorry about your dad."

"Thank you. It was a long time ago."

But not so long ago that it didn't impact her present.

He stood. "I'll walk you to the car."

"There's no need."

"Sure, there is," he assured her. "Your mother will wonder about us if I don't."

"Oh, I guess you're right."

When they reached her mother's car, Roberta got into the driver's seat. Julianna was already in the back seat next to Casey in a child's safety seat.

Ryder opened the passenger door for McKenzie. "Bye, honey. Have fun."

Glaring at him while she climbed into the car, McKenzie's nose crinkled with displeasure at his use of a pet name. "No name calling, remember? I've told you I prefer you to use my name."

"I'll keep that in mind. Have a great time with your mother." He fought chuckling as he leaned forward and pressed a quick kiss on the side of her mouth. One not meant to be full of passion, but not so quick as to just be a peck, either.

"I...uh, thank you. I will." Obviously flustered by his kiss, she gave him a hesitant look. "You're sure you're going to be okay with Jeff while we're gone?"

Although he shouldn't be, he was pleased that his kiss had thrown her off-kilter. "I'll be fine."

Mostly, he believed he told the truth.

"So, tell me about this hot new boyfriend none of us have heard anything about."

McKenzie blinked at her cousin Reva.

They'd barely been at the bridal shop ten minutes. She supposed she should be grateful the question hadn't been the first thing out of Reva's mouth.

Not that her mother hadn't grilled her about Ryder the entire drive into town before dropping her and Julianna off at the dress shop, then heading on to Reva's mother's house to help with whatever Aunt Jane needed.

Then again, it could be worse.

Reva and her family could be grilling her about Paul and not believing her when she said he was ancient history.

"This weekend is about your love life, not mine," she reminded her cousin, eyeing her reflection in the mirror. Although a little snug around the bosom, the bridesmaid dress fit perfectly otherwise.

Reva laughed. "So, true, and I don't mind at all being the center of attention."

Just as well as her beautiful cousin had always held that honor, even in high school. Men had always thrown themselves at her, had done all they could to hold her attention, and it had always been Reva who'd bored with her relationships and ended them.

"But my love life is old news around here," Reva insisted, fanning her face as the seamstress made a last-minute adjustment to her wedding dress. She'd lost weight and wanted the bodice tightened a smidge. "Tell us about yours."

"Not much to tell," she admitted, still going with the truth as much as possible. "Ryder and I work together and have just recently started dating."

Reva's brow arched. "Yet you invited him to come home with you?"

"Of course, I brought him." She hoped she inflected her tone with just the right amount of "duh." "If you were dating a gorgeous pediatric cardiothoracic surgeon, wouldn't you have invited him?"

"If I were dating that man, I'd never leave home," Julianna spoke up from where she fiddled with tying a ribbon on Casey's head in a big bow. "I almost ditched you gals so I could stay at Aunt Roberta's just to drool over him."

McKenzie suppressed a giggle. She'd have to tell Ryder as he'd likely get a kick out of the comment.

"It says a lot about how he feels for you that he was willing to fly across the country to come to a wedding," Reva insisted, keeping her arms held up so the seamstress could work. "Most men hate weddings."

"Ryder isn't most men." So true. Just look at what she'd put him through so far and he'd not uttered one word of complaint.

Instead, he'd been…wonderful.

"It's serious, then?"

If only.

Now where had that come from?

Getting involved with Ryder for real was not what she needed. Hadn't the past taught her anything? Did she really want to get involved with him just so he could dump her down the line, too?

Sensing every woman in the bridal shop's eyes focused on her, including little Casey's, McKenzie hesitated. If she said yes, her family really would be pushing her and Ryder down the aisle.

ranged limo that would take her cousin wherever she needed to go that day.

"She loves it, and you know it. She's been looking forward to this day my whole life."

"As have you," McKenzie reminded her. "I can recall many a time you played dress-up with curtain sheers as your pretend veil."

"Ha. We had fun, didn't we?"

Yes and no. Reva had always been the bride during their play. Never McKenzie. Perhaps that had been a sign of things to come?

"I should have borrowed some of Mom's old curtains for tomorrow, eh?" Reva giggled.

"I seriously doubt that," McKenzie mused, having seen her cousin in the gorgeous dress at the bridal shop.

"Maybe she'll pull them out for you to use," Reva teased.

Wondering at her own botched relationships, McKenzie snorted. "I have no need for curtain sheers or a wedding veil."

"Who knows? Maybe this hot doc, as Aunt Roberta called him, will be the one to change your mind and finally get you to the altar."

Which was what she'd wanted her family to think. That Ryder was crazy about her and she wasn't alone in Seattle.

She arched a brow. "Mom called Ryder a hot doc?"

Reva nodded. "As did Julianna. She said sh

If she said no, then they'd either think she was crazy or that Ryder wasn't that interested.

"It's too early to say." She didn't meet any of their curious gazes as she went back to looking at herself in the mirror. "Do you think we should let the bust out just a little?"

The shop keeper gave a horrified look from where she worked on Reva's dress. "Absolutely not. It's a perfect fit. You want it a little snug to hold everything in place."

There was that. McKenzie stifled a smile as the conversation turned back to the wedding.

That is, until after she was out of the bridesmaid dress and back into her own clothes and Reva tackled her.

"I'm so glad you're here. I've missed you so much." Reva pulled her in for a hug. "And don't even think you've been gone so long that I didn't recognize what you did earlier. Some time before I say I do tomorrow, you and I are going to have a big talk about your new guy. I can't wait to meet him tonight."

McKenzie hugged her cousin. "I've missed you, too."

She had. They'd been so close.

She could blame no one but herself that they no longer were, as she'd been the one to stay away.

Because she couldn't stand the thought of being in an airplane? True, but had that been the main reason she'd not come home?

Was it possible she'd been a tad jealous of her cousin? That she'd jumped at the residency in Seattle to step out of her beautiful cousin's shadow and the pity her family had been dishing out over McKenzie's breakup with Clay?

"I wish you'd gotten to come home for my bridesmaid party last weekend." Reva giggled at the memory. "We had so much fun peddling around Nashville."

"Getting drunk on a bicycle bar isn't necessarily my idea of a good time." Realizing she sounded condescending, she added, "You know I never liked riding a bicycle."

"Come on." One of the bridesmaids hurried them. "If we don't get a move on, we're going to be late for our manis and pedis."

McKenzie glanced at her nails. Her cousin had a flair for gorgeous nails and was always posting a pic on social media of some fantastic manicure with elaborate designs. McKenzie did well to keep hers trimmed and had thought she'd done great with the French manicure she'd taken time for earlier that week. She cared nothing about having her nails redone, but this weekend wasn't about her. So she smiled and went with the flow.

In the middle of their morning of pampering, everyone chitchatted about the wedding, about where Reva thought they'd go on their honeymoon as her husband-to-be had kept it a surprise.

On cue, a courier arrived and presented Reva with a jeweler's box.

"Oh, my goodness!" Reva exclaimed, reading the card out loud, then pulling out a gorgeous diamond bracelet.

"He's so romantic," one of the bridesmaids cooed.

"You're so lucky," another said.

Reva was lucky. Lucky in love. Lucky in life. Always had been. Not once had her cousin ever been dumped.

Reva was wonderful. Why would any man dump her?

Was McKenzie that unwonderful that every man dumped her?

McKenzie bit into her lower lip, chiding herself for the green she'd just felt rush through her veins. She was happy for her cousin. Ecstatic. Just that it would have been nice to have had a little of that lucky at love along the way herself.

They were served champagne and strawberries. McKenzie rarely drank but emptied her glass during her pedicure.

By the time they went to meet the guys for a late lunch at Reva's mother's, McKenzie couldn't decide if she was starved or tipsy. Or both.

"Cooking for everyone on the day before your wedding was a lot for Aunt Jane to take on."

Reva laughed as they piled into the prear-

almost fainted when she walked in on him in the bathroom this morning."

McKenzie grimaced. "That sounds much worse than what it was. Ryder was completely dressed and had just finished brushing his teeth. It wasn't as if she caught him in his skivvies."

"Whatever it was, he flustered her enough she texted to tell me. She said his chest and abs were perfection."

"Yeah, well, compared to your brother, most men's abs would be considered perfection," McKenzie teased. "But Ryder is hot."

She'd have said so a month ago, but just how much so hadn't registered.

Or if it had, she'd just not paid any attention because of Paul and thinking her future was all neatly tied up.

How wrong she'd been.

Ryder, Jeff and a couple of kids paused from tossing the football back and forth on Jeff's mother's front lawn to watch the ladies pile out of the limousine.

"Hello, Hot Doc," McKenzie greeted him.

Ryder's brow lifted. He was even more surprised when she wrapped her arms around his neck and kissed him.

A kiss that was meant for the benefit of their avid audience, one of whom let out a wolf whistle.

Not a problem. Ryder kissed her as if he'd been longing to do so his whole life.

Maybe he had.

When she pulled back, smiled up at him with eyes that were a bit glassy, he grinned down at her.

"Miss me much?"

"Bunches. Couldn't you tell?"

He leaned in so the others couldn't hear. "How much champagne have you had?"

"Not nearly enough," she answered, smiling at him as if she thought he was the greatest thing ever.

He knew it was pretend, but her look was getting to him. Did she ever realize what she was doing? That she was on the rebound and that messed with her emotions? Made her more vulnerable?

"But I did have a couple glasses of champagne while getting my nails done."

She held her fingers out for his inspection.

Knowing they were still the center of attention, that all the women had paused on their way into the house to watch them instead, Ryder took her hand in his and lifted it to his mouth, placing a kiss on each fingertip.

"You're good," McKenzie praised, a bit breathy.

"I'm just getting started."

Which was the truth. For whatever reason McKenzie felt the need to be part of a couple in front of her family and wanted him to act crazy about her.

Kissing her, looking into her eyes, did make him crazy. He was playing a dangerous game. One where he was liable to get burned if he wasn't careful.

Because he wanted McKenzie and feeling her desire during their kiss, as she looked up at him, was playing havoc with his resolve to protect himself.

"I can't wait to see how you finish."

Havoc.

"Are you flirting with me, McKenzie?"

Her cheeks flushed. "Is that not okay?"

The vulnerability in her question about undid him, about made him forget his need to protect himself and instead dive headfirst into wiping away all her self-doubts. He'd like to get a hold of Paul and every other man who'd ever hurt her.

"Okay, that's enough of that," Reva interrupted them, having obviously been ignored for as long as she was willing. "Introduce me to your fellow, Kenz."

McKenzie's cousin was a beautiful woman and had a smile that drew a person in. But Ryder's gaze quickly returned to McKenzie, saw that she was watching him closely for his reaction to her cousin.

"I've heard a lot about you today, Dr. Andrews," the bride-to-be claimed, her smile genuine, as was the hug she surprised him with. "We're all glad you're here."

When Ryder's gaze cut back to McKenzie's she was no longer smiling, or even looking at him. Instead, she seemed bored with the conversation, and mumbled something about finding lunch.

From the lush trees along the edge of where the wedding would take place, Ryder watched the groom and his men line up in front of the wooden archway that would be further decorated with fresh flowers prior to the wedding the following day.

The women, including McKenzie, were to the back of the garden area set up to seat around two hundred people. The trees lining the area provided natural shade and a sense of privacy from the outside world.

A wedding coordinator with a clipboard was instructing and positioning everyone in the wedding party where she wanted them to stand during the ceremony.

Reva was getting married at an old plantation house that had been converted into a wedding venue. The sprawling white farmhouse with its white columns in front and wraparound porch were impressive, but it truly was the scenery around the house and rustic-looking barn that had been built as a reception hall that made the place. Rolling green hills dotted with sprawling oaks, the bluest sky he could recall ever seeing, flowers of all varieties, and a flowing stream that ran along one side of the property.

"Now, ladies," the wedding coordinator continued snapping orders. "I want you hidden back behind these terraces until after the music starts tomorrow."

She put each bridesmaid where she wanted them, had them pretend to hold their bouquets. Then, at designated points in the song, she sent each woman toward the podium where the groom and his men waited.

McKenzie was the second bridesmaid out from where the bride would take her place after all six women had made their way to the front.

McKenzie never looked toward Ryder during her jaunt down the aisle. She just stepped up front to where the wedding coordinator had told her to go, stood holding her pretend bouquet, and kept her gaze trained toward where the other bridesmaids came down the aisle one by one until it was time for Reva to make her grand entrance.

It might be only a rehearsed ceremony, but McKenzie's cousin's appearance garnered everyone's attention, including her groom's, as if she were truly making her grand entrance.

Ryder hadn't met Jeremy yet as the groom and his groomsmen had spent the day on their own adventures. The smile on his face was genuine, as was the love in his gaze when it landed on his bride.

McKenzie was also smiling, but something was off. Ryder wasn't sure it was something anyone else would pick up on, but the way she held her body, the way her smile didn't reach her eyes tugged at everything in him, making him want to go wrap her in his arms and promise to make right whatever was bothering her.

He wouldn't be doing that. At least, not for real.

The couple ran through a mock ceremony with the wedding coordinator stopping them time and again to redirect anything not exactly as she and the couple had previously discussed. When they'd finished and the last of the wedding party had exited the area, she clapped her hands and the handful of people sitting in the pews followed suit.

"Now, this time, we'll run through without interruptions," the coordinator instructed. "If you mess up, just keep going as if this is the real deal. No stopping. Pronto."

The petite woman might have been a drill sergeant in a previous life.

As everyone was resuming their previous places, Ryder moved to one of the pews near the front. Several family members and friends of the wedding party sat in the area, chatting while they waited for the rehearsal to begin again.

"You must be McKenzie's Dr. Andrews."

Ryder glanced up at the man who slid into the pew next to him and nodded.

The man stuck out his hand. "I'm McKenzie's big brother, Mark."

Ryder shook the man's hand. "Ryder."

"I grilled her on you over the phone, but she didn't have a lot to say. Just that I'd like you. She said that about the last guy, too."

"You planning to grill me now to see if you have better luck?" Ryder guessed.

The man gave him a stare down that belonged on a certified interrogator. "It's a big brother's job to look out for his little sister. For the record, she was wrong. I didn't like the last guy."

"Fair enough, and to be honest, I wasn't crazy about him, either," Ryder admitted, earning a quick snort from McKenzie's brother. "What do you want to know?"

"How long have you been seeing my sister?"

"A few weeks."

"Yet she brought you to Tennessee to meet her family? That seems fast."

"Bringing me here may be why she's with me at all," he admitted, sticking with the truth. "I got the distinct impression coming alone wasn't an option she was willing to accept."

Her brother studied him. "You might be right. My mom worries about her."

"As does her brother?"

"Yeah, he does, too, although she's seemed happy enough when I've visited Seattle."

"You get out to see her often?"

"A few times a year. Enough to have my opinions on the guy you replaced. Good riddance."

Ryder waited for him to say more.

"I'm glad she finally saw the light."

Ryder wouldn't correct his assumption that McKenzie had ended the relationship. He'd made the same mistake.

"All of which worked to my advantage," Ryder acknowledged. "If she'd been happy with the last guy I wouldn't be in Tennessee."

"True that."

Both men turned to watch McKenzie slowly make her way up the aisle to the front. When she passed them, her gaze met Ryder's, lingered a moment, then lit on her brother and she grinned.

Ryder almost thought she was going to bail on the wedding procession so she could fling herself at her brother, putting to rest any notion that the two weren't close.

The wedding party went through another mock ceremony, without the bride and groom saying actual vows, then exited as they would the following day.

Ryder wasn't surprised when McKenzie came barreling toward them and flung her arms around her brother.

"Mark! I didn't know you were here."

"Hey, squirt. Miss me much?"

"How embarrassing?" She wrinkled her nose. "Do. Not. Call. Me. That."

He laughed. "Outgrown your nickname?"

"That has never been my nickname. Only you have ever used it and I've always hated it."

Ryder watched the interplay between siblings and could see the closeness that as an only child he'd never experienced. Would he and Chrissy have shared such a bond if she'd lived? He'd have done anything for the chance to know.

Turning her big green eyes toward him, McKenzie smiled and unlike earlier, her smile was real. "Ryder, let me introduce you to the bane of my childhood and for the record if you ever call me squirt, you're history."

Her brother arched a brow. "That sounds painful on a lot of different levels."

"Having you for a brother was painful." But McKenzie was laughing as she said it.

The wedding coordinator clapped her hands and called for everyone to head toward the rehearsal dinner hall.

"As that woman is the bane of my present," McKenzie sighed. "She is so organizing."

"It's her job. Dealing with bridezillas day after day, no doubt she has to be," Mark suggested.

"Reva isn't a bridezilla."

On cue, their cousin burst into tears and sat down on one of the pews.

Mark gestured to their cousin. "You sure?"

"Positive, but that's my calling card to go check on her." She gave her brother a hug, then turned to walk away, and as if an afterthought, turned back, stood on her tiptoes, and kissed the corner of Ryder's mouth.

That was twice she'd kissed him. Once had been for the benefit of the women watching her greet them. That one must have been for her brother because Ryder wasn't sure anyone else had been paying them the slightest heed.

He wasn't complaining. This pretend boyfriend gig came with amazing perks.

Their eyes met, held.

"Sorry you keep getting abandoned."

"You can make it up to me later," he teased.

Her eyes widened with surprise, then after a nervous look toward her brother, she slowly smiled. "We'll see."

Both men watched her rush over to the bride-to-be and kneel next to her, along with the groom and two other bridesmaids.

"That was interesting," Mark mused.

"Your cousin having prewedding nerves?"

"My sister having pre-you nerves," Mark clarified. "Despite the fact my mother threw you in the same bedroom, you've not had sex, have you?"

Leaning back a little, Ryder eyed the man. "With all due respect, whether I have or haven't had sex with McKenzie really isn't your business."

Mark laughed and play punched Ryder's shoulder with a little more zest than just for fun but not meant to truly inflict much pain. More of a warning shot.

"For the record," he cautioned. "Everything to do with McKenzie is my business. I wouldn't take kindly to anyone hurting her."

Admiring McKenzie's brother for his protectiveness of her, Ryder nodded. "Noted, but I don't foresee that being a problem."

After this weekend of pretense, they'd likely go back to rarely seeing each other.

"Also, for the record," Mark continued, his eyes glittering as if he was about to impart great knowledge, "that wasn't boredom flashing in my sister's eyes just then."

Ryder's heart pounded harder than usual at her brother's observation. She was just acting, keeping up the pretense, he tried to tell himself, but didn't believe.

Which meant he needed to be all the more diligent in keeping their boundaries in place when they were alone.

He watched as she wiped a tear from her cousin's now-smiling face. Within seconds, bride and groom were hugging and McKenzie was shooing everyone still there to leave.

"Come on. Let's go find some of this overpriced food," Mark told him as McKenzie rejoined them, giving them curious looks as if wanting to know what they'd been discussing.

"Sounds good." Ryder placed a possessive hand on McKenzie's lower back as they headed in the direction the others had gone. "I'm starved."

He'd meant for food and not McKenzie, right? But the smile she was giving him had him wondering if he was just fooling himself, if he'd just been fooling himself from the beginning, that he could spend a weekend with McKenzie and it all be pretend.

CHAPTER EIGHT

MCKENZIE HADN'T THOUGHT about how much Ryder would have to be alone due to her duties as part of the wedding party.

Now, for instance, she was seated at the wedding party table rather than next to him for the rehearsal dinner.

Fortunately—or unfortunately—her brother had taken it upon himself to keep Ryder entertained.

Or perhaps her brother was entertaining himself at her expense.

Certainly, Mark had taken great pleasure in torturing her throughout their childhood and teen years.

She also knew her big brother would feel it his obligation to thoroughly interrogate Ryder and no doubt already had. What was Ryder telling him?

Or worse, what was Mark telling Ryder?

She shot them a worried glance.

Both men looked relaxed, deep in conversation, and to be enjoying the moment. Mark threw his head back with laughter at something Ryder said.

Interesting. Mark and Paul had gotten along okay enough when Mark had flown into Seattle and they'd all gone to dinner. But she couldn't recall them ever sharing any laugh-out-loud moments. She'd always thought they mostly tolerated each other for her sake.

"Reva's not the only lucky woman here tonight."

Surprised at the comment, McKenzie glanced toward Callie.

Yes, she was lucky Ryder had agreed to this pretense. She almost felt guilty that he had and was being subjected to her family's questioning, guilty that she was using him to stave off pity and perhaps to curb her jealousy at her cousin's good fortune.

Ugh. She hated that seeing Reva had brought a jealousy to surface that she'd not acknowledged she'd had.

"Is he as good in bed as he is to look at?"

McKenzie's gaze went back to Callie. Her high school friend watched Ryder with hungry eyes, probably the way McKenzie had been looking at him that morning when he'd stepped back into her room after his shower.

Yeah, that just-showered look that morning had been outright sexy.

Very sexy.

As had their kiss in Aunt Jane's front yard. Why had she felt the need to lay that one on him? For show in front of her cousin and the other women to say, hey, Reva's not the only lucky one?

If so, how petty of her. But maybe Ryder had been right in thinking the champagne had played a role. Had it given her just enough gumption to kiss him that way, not for show, but because she'd wanted to kiss him and doing so in front of her cousin and the bridesmaids had given her the perfect excuse?

McKenzie swallowed, then, remembering Callie waited for an answer, shrugged. "I don't know," she admitted. "We've only been seeing each other a few weeks."

Callie's perfectly drawn-on brow lifted. "Girl, what are you waiting on? I saw that kiss earlier. Hot. Hot. Hot. If that man was within my hands' reach, I'd know everything about that body of his and he'd definitely know every inch of mine."

Um, yeah, that put a few images in McKenzie's head. Images of exploring Ryder's body, of his exploring hers.

Images that should not be in her head.

Because he was a pretend boyfriend, not a real one. Only more and more she hated the pretense, wished Ryder really wanted her, that everything about this weekend was real.

"Leave her alone," Reva ordered, leaning over toward them from where she sat on the other side of Callie. "McKenzie's just getting out of a long relationship. It makes sense that she'd be hesitant to move too quickly even with a man as wonderful seeming as Ryder."

Reva's quick defense shot guilt through her. Reva had always dragged McKenzie along to all the popular places, had always defended her to anyone who said the slightest negative thing. Her cousin was a much better person than she was and deserved to be happy.

And so did she.

McKenzie's gaze shifted back to Ryder. Was there even a chance of their pretense growing into something real?

She'd have to be dead inside not to react to his overabundance of testosterone.

Not to notice how her body came alive when they kissed or even when he smiled at her.

Perhaps that's why she'd gone for the kiss at Aunt Jane's, because she'd needed the surge of energy his kiss shot through her.

What would he say if she told him she found him attractive, both physically and as a person?

Callie gestured toward where Ryder sat and gave a wistful sigh. "Like I said, lucky you. That man there is the perfect solution to forgetting every other man who ever walked the face of the planet."

All three women looked toward Ryder. He must have sensed their gazes on him as he glanced their way, gave McKenzie a slight look of question, then winked.

"Lord help me," Callie said, fanning her face. "If you decide you don't want him, send him my way. I've not just gotten out of a long relationship and have no reservations about letting him rock my world."

McKenzie fought the urge to fan her own face. Ryder's wink did funny things to her insides. Like make them get all warm and squishy.

Warm?

That was like calling a volcanic eruption a lit match.

"I'd mention your brother," Callie continued, "but we both know that would never work since he's gone so much. I'd get lonely and end up making us both miserable."

Had her mother gotten lonely before her father's death? McKenzie hadn't really thought about what her parents' lives were like before her father died. She'd known her mother had gone through numerous relationships. Had she been trying to curb loneliness? Or had Roberta been lonely long before due to the often out-of-town nature of her father's work?

"Is Ryder going with us after we leave here?" Reva asked. "Lunch was fun, but I hope to get a chance to get to know him while y'all are here and tomorrow is going to be busy."

"Just a little busy. It's kind of your big day." McKenzie smiled at her cousin. "But on Ryder, I honestly haven't had a chance to ask him about tonight."

"I feel guilty I monopolized you all day." Reva's painted lips pouted a little. "Then again, Ryder gets you all the time and this is the first time I've seen you in a couple of years so it's only right he has to share."

Point taken. McKenzie would do better on coming home for visits.

Especially now that she knew she could get through a flight without going into full panic attack mode.

"But, seriously, you've done your bridesmaid duty. Go eat your dessert with your guy and Mark," Reva insisted, having caught McKenzie watching the two men talking and laughing together again.

"Sorry." She glanced toward Reva. "You're sure?"

Reva nodded. "Absolutely. We'll catch up when this is over when we're out on the town."

"But we can't stay out too late on the night before your big day," McKenzie reminded her. She wasn't tired at all, but knew she'd feel the time difference come morning.

"We won't. But going out dancing for a couple of hours will be fun. Besides," the bride assured her, "it's not like I'll sleep if I try going to bed early. Not when I'm so wound up."

Probably not, McKenzie admitted, appreciating Reva's okay to leave the bridal party table to go to Ryder and Mark.

"Care if I join you two for dessert?"

"You get kicked out of the wedding party already?" Ryder teased, pulling a chair over for her to sit next to him.

"I think they were worried about leaving you two alone too long and agreed I should come see what was so funny."

Her brother's eyes twinkled. "I've been telling him about that time you ran through the house naked at Christmas."

"Ah, the infamous naked at Christmas story." McKenzie scowled at her grinning brother. "I was two."

"I might have left that detail out," he admitted, not looking a bit remorseful.

"Ignore ninety-nine percent of what he tells you." McKenzie turned to Ryder. "Are you okay with going to the Wild Horse Saloon? Reva wants the whole gang together for one night of fun on the town, even if for just a couple of hours."

Ryder's eyes lit with surprise, but he nodded. "What's a trip to Nashville without a visit to a honky-tonk?"

"Do you line dance?"

Ryder shook his head. "Is it a deal breaker if I say no?"

"Not really," she admitted. Paul had been a lovely dancer, but they'd danced only when attending social events that just happened to have dancing.

"Is Callie still single?" Mark asked. "I noticed her looking this way several times."

"I think so." After all, she had been drooling over Ryder. "But it wasn't you she was looking at."

Mark's gaze met hers and he grinned. "That jealousy I hear in your voice? Afraid she's going to move in on your man?"

"No," she assured him, her chin lifting in defiance of his claim. "Why would I be jealous?"

Why indeed? Because her brother knew her too well and had called her out on it. Right or wrong, she was jealous at the thought of Callie making advances on Ryder.

Ryder reached out to take her hand. "You know, I'm not interested in anyone but you," he added, lifting her hand to his lips and pressing a kiss to her fingertips.

Although she knew the gesture was just for show, electricity shot through her as she stared into his eyes.

Electricity and a desire so strong for his words to be real that her knees weakened. Pretend boyfriend Ryder was better than any real boyfriend she'd ever had.

If only he really was her boyfriend and had meant what he'd said.

He didn't, but she was thankful he was here, that his generosity had given her a peaceful visit home.

She rewarded him with a smile, then, giving

in to whatever that volcano-like warmth inside her was, she leaned in, meaning to press a kiss to his mouth.

"McKenzie!"

Pausing mid-pucker, she glanced toward the direction she'd heard her name called from.

Across the room, an elderly man was lying on the floor with several people huddled over him. Jeremy's uncle Daniel!

McKenzie and Ryder rushed over to where he lay. "What happened?"

"We're not sure. One minute he was talking and the next he went pale, then collapsed to the floor."

Jeremy's uncle and aunt had come over to her soon after they'd arrived and given her a big hug, asking her about her life in Seattle, and saying how proud they were of her and her accomplishments. Now, the sweet man in his early sixties was unconscious.

"He's breathing, but shallow," Ryder told her from where they stooped over him.

They loosened his shirt buttons and Ryder bent to listen to his chest.

"His heartbeat is bradycardic."

"Pulses are faint, thready," she added, her finger against the unconscious man's left radial artery.

"Is he okay?" someone asked as McKenzie

continued to press her finger against the man's wrist.

"We're not sure," she admitted, propping his feet up onto a nearby chair to increase blood flow to his heart. "Has he ever blacked out before? Any known health problems?"

She was used to dealing with kids but had done multiple adult rotations during her residency. Some things were basic medicine. This was one of them.

"Diabetes, high blood pressure, high cholesterol," an older woman began spouting out. His wife looked as if she might collapse herself any moment.

"He had a stent placed in his right coronary artery a few years back but has done well since that time. I don't recall him ever having passed out, not even before his stent."

Had the stent placed in one of the main arteries supplying his heart with oxygenated blood become blocked again?

"Grab my purse," she ordered Callie, for the sole reason she was the first person McKenzie made eye contact with when she glanced up. She had a resuscitation mouth guard in her bag that she carried with her at all times.

Just in case.

She motioned for her brother to help Jeremy's aunt sit down as McKenzie dialed 911. Regardless of why Uncle Daniel had passed out, he needed a full medical workup as his risk factors were high. They needed to get an ambulance on the way STAT.

"Do you have his blood sugar meter with you?"

It was unlikely the man's sugar had bottomed out since they'd just eaten, but anything was possible.

Ryder had leaned down and was pressing his ear against the man's chest to listen to his heart sounds.

"I have one in my purse," someone else said, grabbing her bag and dumping the contents onto a nearby table so she could quickly hand over a clear bag that held a glucometer, a tube of test strips, some lancets and a few disposable gloves.

"Daniel," she said to the unconscious man just in case he could hear her. "I'm going to check your blood sugar. In just a minute you're going to feel a stick in your finger."

With her cell phone held between her shoulder and her ear, McKenzie reported his status to the dispatcher while she slipped on a glove, pulled the protective cover off one of the lancets and poked the tip of the man's finger. Taking one of the test strips, she pressed the edge to the drop of blood.

Within seconds, the machine flashed with the reading.

"Two hundred and sixty-one." Much too high, but not the cause of the man's syncope.

What worried McKenzie the most was his lack

of response to her sticking him with the needle. He'd barely made a sound at what should have triggered a pain response.

Her gaze met Ryder's and she knew he was thinking the same thing.

The dispatcher said he had an ambulance on its way and McKenzie handed her phone to someone else to talk to the man so she could focus on the patient.

"Mr. Carter?" Ryder shook the man, trying to get a response. "Can you hear me? I need you to open your eyes."

Nothing.

Ryder rubbed his knuckles across the man's sternum with good force which should have elicited a grimace.

McKenzie wasn't surprised when it didn't since he'd failed to react to the lancet.

She placed her finger over his radial pulse again and couldn't find it.

"Ryder," she said firmly to get his attention, not wanting to alarm everyone crowding around them, but becoming alarmed herself. She moved her fingers to his carotid, searching for a beat in case she'd just missed it, but knowing she hadn't.

Reading her mind, Ryder bent his ear to the man's chest again.

"Mr. Carter?" he repeated, shaking the man vigorously. Nothing.

He checked Daniel's airway, then muttered a

low curse as he pressed his hands over the man's chest and began doing compressions.

Thankful she'd sent Callie to retrieve her purse, McKenzie grabbed the mouthguard, ripped off the plastic covering and gave two breaths.

Ryder counted out loud and McKenzie gave the two person CPR recommended two breaths to his every fifteen compressions.

In between breaths, she checked for a carotid pulse, for any sign he'd resumed breathing.

Nothing.

She and Ryder worked together, keeping the rapid lifesaving rhythm going in hopes of reminding Daniel's body of what it should be doing.

After the fourth set of delivered breaths, her own breath caught.

"There's a pulse! Faint, but it's there," she excitedly told Ryder, relief coursing through her entire being.

"Thank God," someone in the crowd said, reminding McKenzie that they had an audience surrounding them. As she and Ryder had worked, she'd completely forgotten where they were. Everything had faded away except for her and Ryder and their efforts to save the man's life.

McKenzie was thankful, too, for the pulse, but knew they were far from out of the woods. Ryder continued to do the compressions, and as McKenzie bent to give her two breaths, the man finally took one on his own. She waited to see if he was going to take another, didn't like how much time passed and went ahead and delivered two more.

"I hear the ambulance sirens," someone unnecessarily said as the distant wail couldn't be missed.

Now, that was something McKenzie was also thankful for. Daniel needed medical attention fast as she was almost positive he'd had a myocardial infarction.

They continued to assist the man's basic vital functions while they waited on the ambulance to arrive. Time seemed to drag but it couldn't have been more than a minute or two in reality.

As his breathing and pulse were sporadic at best, neither she nor Ryder stopped their cardiopulmonary resuscitation efforts.

Just as the emergency sirens came to a halt outside the building, Daniel opened his eyes.

They were blurred, staring up in dazed confusion. McKenzie wasn't sure they were registering much, if anything, but, oh, how she rejoiced at seeing the flicker of movement quickly followed by his taking a deep gasp of air on his own trailed by another.

"Oh, honey." His wife could apparently no longer stay back in her nearby chair and knelt next to him, leaning over, tearful as she continued to talk almost incoherently. "Love you…so scared… please don't…"

McKenzie could make out only part of her

words they were so muffled with tears, and she felt moisture pricking at her own eyes. How much the woman loved her husband, how scared she was, poured from her shaking body.

McKenzie dealt with a lot of sad things in pediatric cardiology but hadn't dealt with an acute heart attack adult patient since residency. It was unlikely that Ryder had either. He seemed to be taking it all in his stride.

McKenzie stayed crouched next to the man, closely monitoring his vitals. Ryder stood to make room for the emergency medical workers to rush to the patient's side. He began filling them in with who he and McKenzie were and what had happened while the crew completed a quick assessment of their own.

"Daniel, it's McKenzie Wilkes. I'm Reva's cousin and a doctor. We're at Jeremy and Reva's wedding rehearsal dinner," she told him to help ground him to where he was and hopefully help keep him calm. "You passed out and we called for an ambulance. The paramedics are here now. They're going to take you to the hospital to be checked further to find out why you lost consciousness."

"I'm okay," the man mumbled low, garnering everyone's attention at his whispered words and weak attempt at sitting up. "Just my chest feels heavy. Sharp pain."

As if to confirm his words his hands went to his chest.

"Don't try talking," one of the paramedics advised, covering his mouth with an oxygen mask.

Quickly, they had an intravenous line in, and he was being rolled to the ambulance on a wheeled stretcher.

Jeremy's aunt and a couple of other family members stayed close to the stretcher, planning to drive to the hospital. McKenzie and Ryder moved along with the stretcher as well, available in the unlikely case they were needed further, but far enough back as to not be in the way.

Most of the guests followed the procession, watching as Daniel was loaded into the ambulance and as it noisily took off with two cars of family members on its tail. Slowly, the guests began returning to inside the rehearsal dinner venue.

Once they were inside, everyone looked around at each other in an anticlimactic way of not knowing what to do next, their over joyous celebrating from earlier having taken a nosedive at Daniel's scary episode. Did they all just pack up and go to the hospital? Or did they proceed with the rehearsal dinner and afterward plans as if nothing had happened to keep from spoiling Jeremy and Reva's rehearsal?

Apparently knowing everyone would look to the bride for guidance, Reva took a deep breath.

Pride filled McKenzie as her cousin spoke.

"Anyone who wants to go on to the hospital, please do. No worries about us. As long as Uncle Daniel is okay, we'll be fine." She smiled at the crowd. "We'll finish here, pack up the leftover food and send it back to Aunt Roberta's house for anyone staying or visiting there to munch on over the weekend. Then, we'll check on Uncle Daniel before we decide whether or not to cancel the rest of our plans."

"Not our wedding plans," Jeremy quickly clarified, shooting his bride-to-be a concerned look. "Regardless of what happens, those plans are noncancelable because I'm marrying you tomorrow."

He lifted her hand to his lips and pressed a kiss there.

A collective sigh resounded across the room, McKenzie's included. Another ping of jealousy also hit her.

Had Paul ever looked at her that way? She wondered. With such love shining in his eyes?

If so, he hadn't for some time.

She'd been so caught up with her career that she hadn't noticed. Or maybe, she hadn't wanted to notice that Paul was no longer enamored of her.

Nor had she noticed that she hadn't been head over heels in love with him. She'd cared deeply for him, had been content with the life she'd believed they'd have together, but had she been with

Paul to appease her worried family and fallen into habit rather than love?

When she got back to Seattle, she was going to find more balance in her life. Hadn't she moved to Seattle because she'd loved walking along the pier? Loved feeling the wind in her face and the sea breeze filling her soul? Because she loved just meandering through Pike Place Market people watching and browsing the goods? And always she'd left with a huge bouquet that made her smile each time she saw it in her house? How long since fresh flowers had adorned her kitchen table?

That balance might not include Ryder or any man, but McKenzie planned to make a few changes, including making time to come back to Tennessee at least annually.

Ryder held out his hand toward her, leading her away from where the crowd lingered, discussing what had happened and how calm Reva was about the ordeal.

Glancing toward Ryder, McKenzie's breath caught as it seemed to have started always doing when he came into view. Truly, he literally took her breath away.

Was it just him and his supersized pheromones that made her so aware of how much a man he was, how much a woman she was?

"Are you okay?"

McKenzie blinked at Ryder. "Yes, thank you," she told him and meant it. She really was. Better than she'd felt in weeks. "How did it take me so long to notice what a good man you are?"

Probably because he'd avoided her, and his overt masculinity had made her uncomfortable when patient care required they interact.

"Good question and one I often ask myself. Let's just be glad you finally noticed."

No doubt his words were for their observers' benefit, as were his next actions. He leaned down and pressed a quick kiss to her lips.

Which left her confused. Had she purposely not acknowledged her attraction to Ryder due to her relationship with Paul? Because the uncomfortableness she always felt she now knew to be sexual tension.

She'd be lying if she didn't admit to feeling electrified at where his lips had pressed against hers. And disappointed the kiss hadn't been more than a swift peck.

Because McKenzie wanted to kiss Ryder. For real.

She wanted to do lots of things with Ryder. For real.

CHAPTER NINE

"VINE TO THE right and hold. Right foot step to the right," the dance instructor said via her headset microphone to be heard over the country music playing in the background of the iconic Nashville honky-tonk on Second Avenue.

Jeremy's uncle had indeed had a heart attack with a blockage in the right coronary artery. Upon arrival at the emergency room, he'd immediately been taken to the heart catheterization lab and had the blockage stented. He was stable, in the cardiac care unit for the night, and doing well with several family members waiting for their brief visit that would be allowed every two hours for a few minutes each.

After going back and forth about whether or not to cancel their original plans, the wedding party and their dates had headed to downtown Nashville at Jeremy and Reva's insistence. As they'd wrapped up the rehearsal dinner so early it was barely eight o'clock when they arrived at the hopping venue on Second Avenue.

Luckily, they caught a group leaving and grabbed their vacated table up near the bar. Part of their crew, all guys, were still there, having a beer, and claiming to be holding the table. Ryder, Jeremy and a single brave groomsman had accompanied the women to the dance floor. Ryder wouldn't have minded staying with the guys at the table, but he had to admit, he was enjoying listening to McKenzie sing along with the country song's lyrics while she went through the motions being given by the dance instructor.

She was a good dancer and kept rhythm perfectly with the directions. He suspected she'd already known the dance prior to their fifteen-minute lesson. But her laughter was contagious, and she seemed to be truly relaxed for the first time since they'd arrived.

He could hold his own on a dance floor during a slow song, was passable during faster dances, but he'd been telling the truth when he implied that he wasn't much of a line dancer.

McKenzie had insisted he join her on the dance floor for the class that was just starting as their group arrived and he hadn't had the heart to disappoint her.

Fortunately, he quickly picked up the dance with only a few missteps.

Like now when he went left when he should have gone right, leading to McKenzie bumping into him when he stepped into her dance space.

Which had happened only because he'd been watching her smiling face rather than paying attention to what he was doing.

"Oops!" Laughing, she grabbed hold of his arm to steady herself. Her palm was warm against his skin.

Warm? Warm didn't scorch straight through every layer and singe a man's insides. McKenzie's touch did that, quickening his pulse more than moving to the music had.

He usually tamped down his attraction to her, but they were in a public place. What could it hurt? After all, they were a pretend couple. A little heat sparking between them would add to the show they were putting on for her family.

"Sorry." He grinned down at her although he wasn't sure he was sorry as her fingers lingered on his arm.

"No worries." Rather than let go, she slowly let her fingertips graze over his skin in a light caress.

Shivers ran down Ryder's spine.

What would it feel like if McKenzie ran her fingers that way over his chest? Over his abdomen? If while doing so she looked at him with the light shining so brightly in her big green eyes? If those eyes darkened with desire?

They would. Ryder saw the sexual energy in her eyes when she looked at him. It had always been there, lurking beneath the surface, tormenting him with the knowledge she'd belonged to another.

McKenzie was no longer in her relationship. She looked at him with passion in her eyes.

But Ryder knew all about a woman on the rebound, about how they could project their feelings, how a rebound fling often soothed a deflated ego.

Ryder swallowed the knot forming in his throat.

If anything happened between him and McKenzie, she'd be using him.

The last time a woman had used him he'd been left with a gaping hole in his chest. He refused to go through that again.

But in this moment, dancing with McKenzie, feeling the energy of her laughter, of her sexual energy, remembering anything other than the fact he wanted her seemed impossible.

Oblivious to his thoughts, she leaned toward him and spoke up so he'd hear her over the music. "You're doing great."

Well, he had been until she smiled, her eyes flashing with another spark of feminine awareness, and his feet took on a mind of their own. He stepped into her dance space rather than out of it, again.

Her lips formed an O, then she laughed but kept going through the steps as instructed by the woman moving around the dance floor, giving pointers.

When Ryder bumped into McKenzie a third time, he shrugged as if he didn't know how it had happened.

"Hey, are you doing that on purpose?" She gave a suspicious look, but her eyes were dancing with delight.

Doing his best to maintain a facade of innocence, he asked, "Would I do that?"

Keeping in step, she arched a brow. "Two weeks ago, I'd have said no. That you'd have done anything to move away from me rather than closer. Now…"

She was right. He had avoided her. Because she'd been seriously involved with another man and when he was around her, he'd wanted to toss aside his common sense and make her his. He might have even been successful, but he didn't go after women who had boyfriends. Or women who were on the rebound from a man they'd planned to marry.

He'd learned that lesson with Anna and wouldn't make the same mistake twice.

His gaze met McKenzie's. She looked at him as if she wanted to strip his clothes off and explore every inch of him.

Was it for show because her friends and family were there?

"Now?" he prompted, wanting to hear what she had to say, to see if she'd flirt back, even if only a little, as he rocked his hips forward and held, then shifted to the left, then rocked to the right, keeping time with the music.

"Now?" Her eyes twinkled. "I'm sure you would."

He laughed. "You might be right."

"Might be?" Her gaze was still locked with his.

"You sure you're a beginner?" Reva called from the opposite side of McKenzie, interrupting their banter. "Because you're picking that up awfully fast."

"Hello?" McKenzie play scowled at her cousin. "Did you not just see him almost knock me down half a dozen times?"

Smiling, Reva shook her head and called, "I must have missed that."

Ryder winked conspiratorially at the bride-to-be who was enjoying herself despite the medical drama at her rehearsal dinner. Probably because her husband's uncle was expected to fully recover and might even be released from the hospital the following day so long as nothing unexpected happened between now and then.

"Okay, now, ladies and gentlemen," the dance instructor said. "From the beginning. Let's go."

The music started over and they went through the motions to the decades-old hit about an achy broken heart. They danced and Ryder kept his body in his dance space, rather than invading McKenzie's, although the temptation to bump her just for another touch was strong.

When the song ended, he was glad he had stayed focused on the dance, because, eyes sparkling, mouth curved in a big smile, she wrapped her arms around him in a hug and squeezed.

"That was amazing. You were amazing!"

Her arms around him was amazing. So amazing Ryder felt his resolve melting. In its place was happiness that he was relaxed, away from work, dancing with a beautiful woman who was flirting with him as if she planned other dances, more primal, in her mind.

"Never say you can't line dance again," she warned.

"Pretty sure being able to follow step-by-step instructions doesn't qualify me to say that I can line dance," he pointed out, wondering what she'd say if he just held her in the hug forever?

Her body felt that good.

Like he wanted to hold her body against his for a very long time. Ryder fought to keep his lower half from reacting in an embarrassing way.

Around them, everyone clapped and thanked the instructor. Eyes locked, he and McKenzie parted and did the same.

The band took the stage again and launched into a slow song. Next to them, Jeremy pulled Reva to him.

McKenzie's gaze lowered and she started walking off the dance floor.

"I don't think so," Ryder said, reaching for her hand even as he acknowledged slow dancing with her would do nothing to stop the erection threatening to make itself present. "If I had to line dance then you don't get to run away when I get an opportunity to show off that I don't really have two left feet despite recent evidence to the contrary."

"You're sure?" she asked, looking as if she wanted to stay, but was hesitant, in case he didn't really want to slow dance and she didn't want to force him to stay.

He wanted to hold McKenzie in his arms.

Any excuse would do.

"Positive." He pulled her to him and put his hands at her lower back, holding her close as they began to sway to the country love ballad.

McKenzie's head rested just beneath his chin as they moved in perfect harmony to the song Ryder had never heard before but would never hear again without thinking of McKenzie and this moment.

Without remembering her light flowery smell and warm body next to his wreaking all kinds of havoc with his internal circuitry.

Holding her like this had him wondering what it would have been like had McKenzie been single when he'd arrived in Seattle. What if Paul had never been in the picture? What if he'd never had to tamp down the way she burned his insides and instead could have let her set him on fire over and over.

Her fingers toyed with the hair at his nape. "Thank you, Ryder."

"For not stepping on your toes?" Her fingers in his hair was making his feet happy enough to walk on air.

"That," she agreed, brushing her thumb slowly across the back of his neck, "and everything else. For coming with me this weekend, for being so great at the rehearsal dinner, for saving Jeremy's uncle's life."

"That was a partnered effort," he reminded her, pressing his palm into the curve of her lower back to keep her close. Her body next to his felt good. "You played just as big a role in saving his life as I did."

"Thanks, but I don't think so. You were wonderful. Jeremy's family all think you're a hero. My family, too. Which is great, only..."

"Only?" he prompted.

Her gaze lifted to his and she searched his eyes, making him wonder just how much of his thoughts she'd read, especially when she answered his question.

"None of it is real."

They weren't real, McKenzie reminded herself for the dozenth time in the past five minutes.

Literally, she kept reminding herself, because it was easy to forget they were pretending when Ryder smiled at her with a certain look in his eyes.

Ryder wasn't her boyfriend.

Despite her reminder that had been for herself as much as for Ryder, he was smiling.

Why wouldn't he be? It didn't matter to him that they weren't real, that the sexual tension building between them on the dance floor was a byproduct of proximity, pretense and young, healthy bodies rather than something more.

Her family all bought that they were a real couple.

Only rather than being happy at how well her plan was working, she laid her head back against his shoulder and moved to the music with him in slow, rhythmic movements and fought sighing.

Because they were doing such a good job pretending that they were convincing her, too.

She liked how he held her, firmly against him, but not too tightly.

Being in Ryder's arms, having him hold her next to him, feeling his warm breath against the top of her head, was an experience unlike anything she recalled.

She couldn't remember having her ear pressed against Paul's chest, listening to his heartbeat, or perhaps feeling it against her cheek more than actually hearing the resounding *lub-dub* over the twangy love song, and being so aware of each beat. Of being aware of the strength of the chest she leaned against. Of being so in sync with that rhythm and becoming mesmerized by the tune it played.

Of being so aware of the spicy male scent surrounding her and flashing her back to when he'd stepped into her bedroom fresh from his shower that morning and filling the room with him—his scent, his presence.

Of how her thighs had clenched, her heart had quickened, her throat had tightened.

The song ended and another started, its beat a little faster than the previous song. She and Ryder didn't pull apart, just kept moving to the music.

She closed her eyes.

This feels right.

Only it was make-believe.

Ryder's lips brushed against the top of her head, softly, but she'd definitely felt the caress. Opening her eyes, she caught Reva and Jeremy watching them. Smiling big, her cousin gave a thumbs-up sign.

Down the road, many years from now, she'd tell Reva the truth. Her cousin would understand why she'd wanted Ryder with her. No one wanted to come home for a wedding single, dejected and at her meddling family's mercy.

She might even admit to the green tinging her blood at how Reva's life was so wonderful and to the guilt she felt at her jealousy.

Glancing over at where Jeremy and Reva were hugged up on the dance floor still, her cousin laughing at something he'd said, McKenzie's chest squeezed. That's what she wanted. Someone to love her and laugh with her and want to spend their life with her.

Was that such an impossible want?

"What are you thinking?"

She lifted her head from Ryder's strong chest to look at him. "Nothing, why?"

"You got tense. Everything okay?"

The man was too observant.

Still, McKenzie had no real regrets on bringing Ryder with her. To have come alone would have thrown an ugly wrench into McKenzie's entire visit.

Because of him, this weekend had been fun, exciting and full of self-discovery.

"Just thinking how nice this is, spending unpressured time with my family, getting to know you, dancing with you," she admitted.

"It is nice, but don't forget none of this is real."

No chance of that happening.

"It would be nice if it were, though."

He stiffened against her and she realized they'd stopped dancing, were standing close, and to the casual observer probably just looked to be talking.

Obviously, her last comment had raised his hackles.

Embarrassed that she'd let herself get caught

up in the heated emotions being with him caused, she forced a smile in his general direction.

No worries, Ryder. I know this is only pretense to you.

That's all it had been to her, too. Initially.

Now, she wasn't so sure, which was obviously making him uncomfortable.

She'd save him from having to stress that they weren't real and never would be.

"Now, no more serious talk. Let's have some fun."

Just after eleven Ryder and McKenzie were back at her mother's house. Her cousin Jeff and his family had already called it a night, as had her mother. All the lights were off except the front porch and a couple of night lights.

Mark was still out with the others, saying not to wait up on him as he'd likely find more comfortable sleeping arrangements than the sofa.

Ryder let McKenzie use the bathroom first, wandering around her childhood room to check out the boy band posters adorning her walls. He could just imagine her and Reva blasting the music and singing along at the top of their lungs.

Seeing how close they were, he wondered again why had she chosen to move so far away from her family?

With him, his parents were super successful single children of small families and, with Chrissy's death, he was an only child. There were no big gatherings at holidays or chaotic shared bathrooms. Next to McKenzie's family, his home life seemed quite dull.

He picked up a framed photo off her dresser. McKenzie held a volleyball and Reva was in a cheerleader outfit. They were hugged up like the best of friends, much as they'd been embracing on the dance floor.

When the connecting bathroom door opened, McKenzie had changed into shorts that were barely visible beneath an oversized T-shirt.

His breath caught at the sight of her shapely legs, brushed-out long hair and freshly washed face. She was beautiful.

Brilliant and beautiful.

Sexy as hell.

"Your turn," she offered, unaware of the lust she was unleashing in his body while she hung her dress back onto a hanger in her closet. When she turned, realized he'd been looking at the photo of her and Reva, something flashed in her eyes that struck him as odd.

Then realization hit.

He felt such a fool. How had it taken him so long to figure out the truth?

Then again, he'd been blinded by his own attraction to McKenzie, blinded by her recent breakup with Paul.

Paul had been a rebound relationship.

Ryder set the photo frame back on the dresser. "I like to think I'm pretty astute, but I completely missed what was going on here."

"Oh?" Her gaze lifted to his much as a doe's caught in a headlight.

"I assumed it was something that had happened between you and your family that had you moving to Seattle, but then you all seemed so close that I'd decided I was wrong."

"I never said anything happened to cause me to move to Seattle other than that I fell in love with the city," she reminded him, placing her fists on her hips as she regarded him.

"But," he continued as if she hadn't said anything, "it was you and Reva who had a falling out."

"You're crazy," she accused, but looked away as she busied herself straightening the clothes in her closet. "My cousin and I did not have a falling out."

"I knew you were stressed about coming home, but I got that a wedding is a little more pressure to not be single. Now, it all makes sense. What happened between you and your cousin?"

"Nothing happened."

He wanted her to tell him the truth, rather than him having to pry it from her.

Frustrated, he said, "Something happened. Otherwise I don't think you'd have moved quite so far."

McKenzie didn't meet his eyes. "You're drawing wrong conclusions, Ryder."

"Am I?" His brow lifted, then he shook his head. "I don't think so, but I'll let you think you're deceiving me the way you're deceiving yourself if you really believe that."

She rolled her eyes. "You barely know me, haven't even been in this house twenty-four hours. So, don't you go psychoanalyzing me, Ryder."

"Then you and Jeremy were never a thing? Because my guess is he's what came between you and your cousin."

McKenzie burst out laughing. "Jeremy and I were never a thing. I knew him in school, of course, but he, and every other guy, was crazy about Reva. How could they not be? She's wonderful."

"Then who came between you?"

"No one," she repeated. "I—I was involved with someone during my senior year of high school and into college, but Reva never dated him."

"Did she want to?"

"Not to my knowledge. Clay didn't break up with me because of Reva, Ryder. He left me to take a residency in Boston and I took one in Seattle. End of story."

"How long were you together?"

"What does that matter?" She took a deep breath. "Seven years."

All this time he'd thought it was Paul who was his greatest competition, Paul who he had to worry about being a rebound guy from. Was it actually someone he'd never heard her mention?

"Not that it's any of your business, but Clay and I dated for seven years. We planned to both go to Seattle." She gave a wry snort. "I didn't even know he'd applied for a residency in Boston. My family worried about me going so far away when I was upset about the breakup and wouldn't know a soul. They didn't understand that going to Seattle rescued me from their pity."

"Loving you and wanting to help you through a breakup isn't the same thing as pity."

"How would you know, Ryder? I seriously doubt that anyone pities you. Do you want to know what my biggest issue is since coming home? That I'm freaking jealous of my cousin's happiness. Don't get me wrong. I'm glad she's marrying Jeremy, but what is wrong with me that I can't have a good relationship, too?"

She was standing close to him, glaring up at him with eyes that flashed with anger and hurt.

He didn't want to fight with her and searched for the right words to answer her questions.

Her questions that cut to his very core.

But she wasn't finished, and perhaps hadn't even wanted answers to her questions, but was just shooting words out at him like emotional arrows meant to pierce deep.

"Good for you on figuring out that not only was I dumped by Paul, but also by a man I'd given seven years of my life to thinking we'd someday marry, too." Another self-deriding snort flared from her nostrils. "Obviously, I'm very dump-able."

"You're not very dumpable."

"Right." Seeming to deflate, she gestured toward the bathroom. "Don't you need to change before bed?"

"You mean floor?"

Her gaze narrowed. "I'll gladly take the floor."

"No." He regretted his stupid quip. "I don't want you taking the floor."

She didn't answer, just stood waiting for him to go to the bathroom with her chin lifted.

Which gutted him.

What he wanted more than anything was to wrap his arms around McKenzie and wipe the exhausted, dejected look off her face.

"I'm sorry."

Her chin hiked up a few more notches. "I don't want or need your pity. I'm fine."

Gathering his pajama pants, Ryder crossed the room to the bathroom door, paused a moment as he racked his brain for something to defuse the tension between them.

The last thing he wanted was to upset McKenzie, although he seemed to be doing a good job of doing just that.

"I really am sorry I jumped to conclusions, McKenzie. I wish you'd told me everything. It would have made things make sense."

"No doubt, you're right," she surprised him by saying. "I doubt you've ever been dumped, so how could you possibly understand that I might not have wanted to admit to just how dumpable I am?"

He understood more than she thought. He'd been dumped, had his heart broken and probably even been the recipient of some of that pity she'd mentioned.

"Neither of them deserved you."

"Just go get ready for bed," she ordered, no longer meeting his gaze. "We've got a long day in front of us tomorrow."

When Ryder had finished in the bathroom, he wasn't surprised to see her curled up on the floor, pretending to be asleep.

Fine, let her pretend.

He'd just pretend like he believed her and put her faking it butt up into the bed. Walking over to the bed, he pulled back the covers, as if he was about to climb in, then squatted beside her and slipped his arms beneath her.

"What are you doing?" she squealed as he lifted her from the floor.

"Tucking you in, Sleeping Beauty."

"Put me down." She wiggled in his arms.

"Planning to," he assured her, setting her onto

the bed, then pulling the covers over her body while she stared up at him a bit slack-jawed. "Goodnight, McKenzie. Sleep tight."

She glared at him as if he represented everything wrong in her life.

Maybe he did since she was using him as a shield against having to face those things.

Reaching over, he turned the lamp light out, then took a deep breath.

He'd had to kill the light.

Because looking down at her, her eyes flashing green fire, her lips pursed in anger, his every instinct had been to kiss her.

To kiss her until she was breathless, and her anger burst into flames of desire.

To kiss her until she forgot about Clay.

And Paul.

Any every other man she'd ever cared about.

Ryder wanted to kiss her until she couldn't think about anyone other than him.

His instinct wanted that kiss, wanted all those things, but he wouldn't do any of those things.

The last thing he or McKenzie needed was another rebound relationship destined to end in disaster.

Lying down on the floor, he listened to her breathing go from loud, exaggerated huffs to calmer, even breaths, but he knew she wasn't asleep.

What would she say if he reached up and took

her hand into his? Would she smack it away? Or would she let him hold her hand the way he wanted to hold her?

"I have been dumped."

Silence met his admission.

"I mentioned her to you on the plane. She and I were in Pittsburgh together. I knew she was just coming out of a bad relationship, but I got caught up in a whirlwind romance with her."

Why was he telling her about Anna?

"I was crazy about her. When I started sensing her pulling away, I became more desperate to change her mind." Pain slashed at his chest at the memories of how he'd been used. "Seems she'd started talking to her ex again. They were sleeping together, but she worried about ending things with me because of our research." He paused, took a deep breath. "She resented that she felt she couldn't end things with me and finally she admitted she'd only used me to get back at her ex."

Ryder curled his fingers into his palms, pressing the tips deep into his flesh as he continued. "I was angry at her for not being honest with me. I hated myself for being so stupid and allowing myself to be used, and swore I'd never make that mistake again."

He uncurled his fingers, let out a slow breath. "So, when you accuse me of not knowing what it feels like to be dumped, you're wrong. I know all too well."

McKenzie lay perfectly still in the bed, but he knew she'd heard ever word he'd said, that she was processing his admission.

"For whatever it's worth, they were fools for letting you go."

Silence met him, and he wondered if she'd say anything at all.

Then she softly said, "Seems the world is full of fools."

The pain in her admission punched him. McKenzie was so much more than both men. Ryder couldn't understand why either would have let her go.

"You're better off without them." His words seemed blasé even to him. Just something people said when someone ended a relationship. But his words were true. If the men hadn't cherished McKenzie, had been willing to let her go, she was better off without them. "Surely you recognize that?"

"As you're better off without Anna?"

Had he said Anna's name out loud? Ryder knew he hadn't. But then, one of the things he'd always admired about McKenzie was her sharp mind.

"I am," he acknowledged. He was. Although he hadn't seen it at the time, Anna hadn't been the right woman for him.

Ryder waited for McKenzie to respond, but despite the fact she lay awake for a long time, she never said anything more.

Just lay in her bed, her breathing even, but not to where he thought her asleep.

Which meant what?

He'd done nothing wrong. She'd dragged him into this wedding weekend. He'd had every right to ask about Reva, to think a man had come between her cousin and her.

McKenzie bringing him to Tennessee might have been the best thing for everyone involved. He could see that now.

Everyone, that is, except Ryder, as the last thing he needed was to be a rebound guy, again.

CHAPTER TEN

McKENZIE HAD LAIN awake a long time and once she'd fallen asleep had passed out to oblivion to everything around her.

She'd not heard Ryder get up, get a shower and leave the room, but he wasn't on the floor.

Panic hit.

Had he had enough of this crazy situation and left?

The thought that he might be gone made her head light. *Please don't let him have left.* For so many reasons, she wanted Ryder with her in Tennessee.

Not the least of which was how happy she felt when he was near. How aware she'd become of her body when near him.

He'd been doing her a favor and she hadn't given him all the facts.

He'd been used in the past. Yet, he was essentially allowing McKenzie to do the same, to use him to pretend everything in her life was wonderful when it wasn't.

Why had he agreed to come with her to Seattle?

Thanks to his having blocked her out after

those first few weeks he'd been in Seattle, they barely knew each other.

Yet, truth be known, Ryder knew more about her than any person in Seattle, including Paul.

She owed Ryder an apology. He'd had every right to ask about her life since she'd dragged him right smack dab in the middle of it.

She'd gotten so angry at him the night before, but in truth, she'd been angry at herself, ashamed of herself, and perhaps having a bit of a pity party for herself, which she detested.

Please let Ryder forgive me.

Getting out of bed, she paused long enough to go in the bathroom to brush her teeth, then went searching for him, wandering into the kitchen where she found her mother, Aunt Myrtle, Julianna, and a few cousins spread out around the kitchen.

Ryder wasn't there!

Her heart sank, her mind racing ahead to returning to Seattle to find him, to talk to him, to make him listen.

"Good morning," her mother greeted from the sink where she washed dishes.

"Morning," McKenzie said back, heading straight for the coffee pot. She needed coffee. Then she'd figure out her next move.

"Coffee's fresh," Julianna assured her from

where she lorded over her three-year-old, trying to make Casey eat. "And dark."

"Perfect."

"Your fellow is out in the garage helping Mark and Jeff figure out what's wrong with my car," Aunt Myrtle informed her, not looking up from her crossword puzzle.

Ryder was still there? He hadn't left? Thank God!

The emotions flooding her that he hadn't left had her grabbing hold of the countertop, sending a happy tremble down her spine.

"I wondered where he was," she said to no one in particular, just needing to let some of the joy inside her escape.

"They all went out there right after Myrtle arrived and complained about the noises her engine was making," her mother said, rinsing a mug and placing it onto a towel.

Did Ryder know anything about working on cars? Did her brother and cousin, for that matter?

What did it matter so long as Ryder was still there?

"What's wrong with your car, Aunt Myrtle?" McKenzie asked as she poured a steaming cup of coffee, then added just the right amount of cream and sugar.

"If I knew, I wouldn't need them to figure that out."

Julianna glanced up from where she fed her youngest, her gaze meeting McKenzie's. Both women suppressed a smile at their quirky great-aunt.

"Hope they get it figured out. I've a pinochle game next week I'd hate to miss."

McKenzie leaned back against the countertop, sipping her coffee, taking in the commotion around the kitchen. Home. The sights, the smells, the feeling. She was home.

"You want me to help with the dishes, Mama?"

"No, thanks, honey. I'm about finished." Her mother placed a cup in a drainer, then dried her hands on a dishtowel.

At that moment, Ryder, Mark and Jeff came into the house. All of their hands covered in grease, and they were talking and laughing among themselves.

McKenzie's breath hung in her throat at seeing Ryder, at hearing his voice, his laughter. Thank goodness she'd not had coffee in her mouth, or she'd have possibly choked.

Oh, Ryder, I'm so sorry about last night.

Not that he could read her mind, or had even looked her way, but she willed him to know how sorry she was and to forgive her.

"Mark!" her mother squealed when her son moved toward her as if he was going to give her a hug.

"Don't touch a thing!" Jeff's wife added.

"Y'all don't look ready to go to a wedding," Aunt Myrtle said matter-of-factly from where she frowned at them over the top of her newspaper.

"Dibs on the bathroom," Jeff called, heading down the hallway.

Mark walked over to the kitchen sink, picked up the dishwashing detergent and squirted a big glob in his hand.

"Mom, I'm going to scrub up, then hop in your shower."

"Don't you go making a mess in my bathroom," she warned.

While all the commotion was going on, McKenzie had kept her gaze pinned on Ryder. Had held tightly onto her coffee mug because her hands shook.

Because she could tell he was avoiding looking at her, as if he didn't know what to expect when he did.

When their gazes met, her chest fluttered, reminding her she owed him an apology for the night before.

For involving him in this whole mess.

"I'm sorry," she mouthed, giving a small smile as a peace offering.

From where he continued to stand just inside the doorway, he half-smiled back.

Oh, heavens. Everything was going to be okay. He hadn't left. He'd smiled back. She'd get a chance to tell him all the things she'd thought of while lying in her bed the night before.

She'd get a chance to tell him that when he smiled he cleared the clouds from her world and made her feel as if she were lifting her face into the sunshine.

She'd get a chance to tell him she didn't understand all the things going on inside her, but one thing was glaringly clear. There was nothing pretend about the way her heart contracted because of him, nothing pretend about how seeing him set her libido ablaze, nothing pretend about how she'd trusted him with her deepest secrets the night before.

She put her coffee mug down and gestured to the sink. "Let me help you get clean before my ride to the venue gets here."

His gaze not leaving hers, Ryder stepped up next to McKenzie and held his hands over the recently drained sink.

McKenzie picked up the grease-cutting detergent and squirted some in his palms, turned on the water, and checked to make sure she had the temperature correct. She watched as he rubbed his hands together, scrubbing around his nails, rinsing, then holding his hands out for another round of detergent.

McKenzie obliged, but rather than watch him, this time, she took his hand and a dishcloth and began wiping at the remaining dark spots.

Why was her heart racing at washing his hands? This was ridiculous. But no more so than how the slightest brush of her fingers against his sent shivers over her skin.

Ryder's gaze lifted to hers in surprise, but he didn't say anything, just let her clean his hands.

His strong, talented hands that were capable of saving lives.

Hands that felt good in her own.

Hands she wanted holding hers, touching her, caressing her.

Afraid to look up for fear of what she'd see in his eyes, McKenzie dropped the cloth into the sink, pulled his hands beneath the running water to wash away the suds, and lingered there as the warm water flowed over their hands.

Knowing she needed to convey something of what she was feeling, she laced her fingers with his and held on tight.

Water rinsed over their hands much longer than necessary before McKenzie reluctantly turned to grab a dry cloth.

Ryder turned off the faucet and shook the excess water from his hands. McKenzie wrapped his hands in the towel, patting him dry.

"Thank you."

"You're welcome." Could he see everything bursting within her?

Needing to be sure he knew how much she appreciated him, how sorry she was for how defensive she'd been, she lifted Ryder's hand to her lips and pressed a kiss there.

If he'd looked surprised at her washing his hands, he looked stunned at the kiss. Regardless, he quickly masked it.

"You must have slept well."

"Eventually. I had a lot on my mind," she admitted, going back to massaging his hand with the towel. "You?"

"Same."

Her gaze met his. She sucked in a soft breath, then squeezed his hand. "Sorry if I kept you awake."

He hesitated only a second, then said, "You really need to do something about that snoring."

Her brows V'd as relief filled her at his teasing. "I don't snore."

"Sure, you do. It's quite adorable." He laughed, then pulled her to him, whispering in her ear. "We have a very attentive audience."

Which she had completely forgotten.

Because all she'd been thinking was how happy she was that he was there.

She forced a smile. "Keep up the good pretense."

McKenzie hadn't seen Ryder since she'd left her mother's house. She had spent the remainder of the morning with the rest of the bridesmaids being painted, powdered, curled, sprayed and beautified to the point McKenzie's eyes threatened to cross.

Still, she had to admit the bridesmaids all looked beautiful in their peacock-blue dresses and updos. As should be, none of them compared to her stunning cousin, though.

Reva made a beautiful bride who'd rival any magazine cover.

She'd chosen a slightly off-white form-fitting lace dress with a creamy ribbon at her waist. The neckline hinted at her cleavage but didn't reveal any secrets.

They'd had hundreds of photos taken around the venue, outside. Individual photos. Photos with the bride. Photos with the groom. Photos with the groomsmen. None of the bride and groom together though as they'd gone with the tradition of the groom not seeing the bride on the wedding day prior to her walking down the aisle to him.

Then it was time for the wedding.

"Thank you for being here."

Surprisingly, McKenzie hadn't felt a bit green all day. Probably because she'd been too distracted by thoughts of Ryder and wanting to strangle him that he'd thought she was pretending.

There had been nothing pretend about how she'd felt seeing him walk into her mother's kitchen, how she'd felt holding his hands while she washed them.

She liked him. Crazy that admitting that she liked her pretend boyfriend made her happy, but it did.

It also made her crazy.

Ryder had been used in the past, had been hurt.

Smiling at Reva, hoping her cousin was always as happy as she was at that moment, McKenzie hugged her. "I love you, Reva. I wouldn't have missed your wedding for the world."

She meant it, too. She was grateful for her cousin's wedding, for it forcing her home, for it forcing her to evaluate a lot of things about her life and choices.

For pushing her into convincing Ryder to come to Tennessee.

No matter what happened, she was grateful she'd gotten to know him, gotten to experience how it felt to kiss him.

If those had been his pretend kisses, she could only imagine what his real ones were like.

"Don't make me cry," Reva ordered, air-kissing McKenzie's cheek.

The music hit the note where McKenzie was to come out. She made her way, keeping her smile bright for the ever-present photographer.

Trying to keep the appropriate pace and not fall on her face, she walked down the aisle.

Her gaze sought where she knew Ryder would be sitting, spotted him, and she smiled.

A smile that came automatically and naturally.

A smile that came from deep inside.

A smile he returned and that even though it might be for show truly made her feel better.

Despite his having put on a good show that morning for anyone who might be looking their way, she couldn't help but wonder if that was all he'd been doing.

What if, unlike her, he hadn't started to have real feelings? Real desires?

Callie joined her in the wedding lineup, then the music changed to what every moment of the day had been building up to. Every wedding guest stood, turned to look toward where the bride would soon appear.

And then Reva was there.

McKenzie's heart filled with pride at her beautiful cousin's obvious love and happiness as she made her way down the aisle to her waiting groom.

The wedding ceremony went perfectly, with the groom soon kissing his bride.

McKenzie was paired with a groomsman, and arms linked, they walked back down the aisle with the photographer snapping away as they did.

They posed for photos that included the bride and groom, then were soon dismissed while the photographer took shots of just the bride and groom.

Once inside the reception hall, McKenzie immediately sought Ryder.

"Looking for someone?"

"Oh!" She spun at his voice, almost losing balance as she stared into his honey eyes.

"Sorry." He grabbed her elbow, steadying her. "I didn't mean to startle you."

"Were you waiting on me?"

"Something like that."

He must have been, otherwise, he wouldn't have been so close to the door because she'd barely made it inside the reception hall.

Just looking at him filled her with such jitters, with such a need to talk to him, away from the crowd.

"I—I don't want to stay here, Ryder."

His brow lifted. "You want to go back to Seattle?"

"Yes, but that's not what I mean." She grabbed his hand and pulled him toward the door she'd just come through. "I need some fresh air."

"Even though you just came from outdoors?"

"Work with me here," she ordered as she took off in the opposite direction of where the bride and groom were still snapping shots.

She walked until she came to a gazebo that was laced with deep red knock-out roses. Inside the gazebo was a bench and just beyond it was a small gurgling creek.

"Wow," she breathed. "Beautiful."

"Yes."

McKenzie turned toward him. He'd been looking at her and not the gorgeous scenery.

"I'm sorry about last night, Ryder. I wanted to
tell you this morning, but I overslept and then we
were never alone and… I should have told you
about Clay."

"You could have told me."

She nodded. "I should have. Only…"

"Go on," he repeated.

"Only, you are a gorgeous, successful man.
What sane woman wants to tell you she wasn't
worth hanging on to by any man she's ever
dated?"

"You don't believe that, do you?"

She shrugged. "Not really."

"Wherein lies the problem. Have you ever considered that there were other reasons why your
relationships don't work out?"

McKenzie took a deep breath, stared out at the
pond. "It really is beautiful here, isn't it?"

"Is that how you deal with things you don't
want to deal with? Change the subject?"

"You want me to go into the details of my
breakup with Clay? Or give you all the details
of my breakup with Paul?"

"It's not on the top of the list of conversations
I'd like to have with you, but if it would help you
to talk about it, I'm game."

Why was she getting upset with him again?
She'd spent the entire day planning to let him

know how much she regretted their disagreement the night before.

She winced. "I don't want to talk about any man but you, Ryder. I want to talk about us, about what's happening between us."

His lips pressed to a thin line.

"Don't confuse this weekend with something real, McKenzie. You're on the rebound and that makes everything feel more intense."

She opened her mouth to correct him, but he pulled her to him, silencing her just as she realized someone was nearing the gazebo.

"Is everything okay?"

Reva! McKenzie should have known the photographer would want photos at the gazebo and creek.

Rather than answer her cousin with words, because words failed her, McKenzie placed her hands against Ryder's cheeks, stood on tiptoes and kissed him.

Because if she couldn't tell him with words how she was feeling, maybe she could show him.

It's for show, Ryder reminded himself.

That was the only reason McKenzie was kissing him. Because her cousin, Jeremy and the photographer had walked up on their discussion, and true to everything about this weekend for McKenzie, she didn't want there to be the slightest dark cloud on her cousin's big day.

Ryder should care that he was being used, should pull away. He did care.

But this was what he'd agreed to.

For all intents and purposes, he had agreed to be used.

So, he kissed McKenzie back as if he believed she was kissing him because she wanted to kiss him rather than to reassure their audience who might have picked up on their tension.

He kissed her as if the sweetness with which she caressed his face was a true lover's touch.

"Ahem," the photographer interrupted.

Ryder's gaze locked with McKenzie's, he waited for her to pull away from him. Slowly, she did so, her eyes hazy, her lips plump from their kiss, as she turned toward her cousin.

"Oh, sorry. We just needed a few minutes to ourselves. You know how it is." With that, McKenzie grabbed his hand. "We'll get out of the way."

CHAPTER ELEVEN

"THAT KISS, THOUGH!" Reva cooed later when the wedding party was seated at the front of the reception hall. "I thought smoke was going to start coming out of your ears any moment when we walked up on you at the gazebo."

Fighting rising heat in her face, McKenzie smiled at her cousin. "Ryder is a good kisser."

"Have you slept with him yet?" Callie asked.

McKenzie didn't answer.

"Girl, what are you waiting for? You're sleeping in the same room. Please tell me you're not making him sleep on the floor." Callie fanned her face. "That man is hot."

Ryder was hot. He was also not really hers. Kenzie had never slept around, had only ever been with two men. She couldn't just sleep with Ryder because of his close proximity. She needed more than that to give her body to a man.

"I imagine no one makes Ryder Andrews do anything he doesn't want to do," McKenzie answered, glancing over at where Ryder sat with her brother. The two of them seemed to have truly hit it off and were once again deep in conversation.

"He seems a great guy, Kenz," Reva pointed

out. "I hope it's not too long before we're celebrating your big day."

McKenzie almost choked on the bite she'd just taken.

"Let's get through your wedding day before we start planning mine." Which might not have been the right thing to say as Reva's eyes widened with delight.

"I knew it."

McKenzie got through her wedding obligations and was grateful when the wedding party were freed from their duties so they could mingle among the other guests.

"Okay, I need all the single ladies," the wedding coordinator announced. "Come on, girls. It's time for the bouquet tossing."

McKenzie reluctantly joined the other single women. Reva met her gaze, winked, then turned to toss the bouquet. Rather than join the scurrying to catch the flowers, McKenzie stepped back, happily letting Callie snatch the bouquet.

When she rejoined Ryder and Mark, the two men shook their heads.

"I'm disappointed. You should have had that bouquet."

"I didn't want that bouquet," she pointed out.

"Okay, gentlemen, it's your turn," the coordinator announced. "Gather up front."

"You don't have to go up there," she told Ryder.

"Sure, I do," he countered, standing, then bending to give her a quick obligatory peck on the lips. "Wish me luck."

Knowing several of the guests around them, including her brother, could hear everything being said, McKenzie smiled. "Go get 'em, Tiger."

When Ryder caught the garter, he held it up like a prized trophy, looked McKenzie's way, and waggled his brows. The crowd loved it and let out cheers.

McKenzie's face burned, but she kept her smile in place.

"Looks like you finally have one wanting to stick around," Aunt Myrtle said from a table over. Her voice was loud and carried to where half the guests in attendance had to have heard, Ryder included. McKenzie blushed.

"Look what I got for you," he bragged, twirling the garter on his finger.

"Hate to break it to you, but perhaps you didn't notice during the bouquet toss, I don't want that."

Grinning, he leaned in close and whispered, "Sure, you do. Everyone here will be busy talking about my catching this rather than you missing the bouquet that practically dropped into your arms. You can thank me later."

That's why he'd caught the garter? Because he was still trying to help her save face?

She'd never met anyone like him. He had no reason to help her, and yet, he was determined to do everything he could to make her look good.

She wanted to hug him. For real.

"Now, congratulate your man."

McKenzie's brows started V'ing together, then she recalled they really were the second most-watched couple at the wedding.

"Congratulations, Ryder." She smiled beatifically, leaned close to his ear and whispered, "You planning to wear that for me later tonight?"

If she'd been trying to leave Ryder speechless, good job.

Because, although he could think of dozens of responses to her comment, he couldn't form the words to say a single one.

Because his brain kept getting stuck on the fact that she'd been flirting with him.

For real.

Self-preservation demanded Ryder keep his guard up.

Because staying away from McKenzie once they were back in Seattle was going to be more difficult.

He'd do it, though.

The wedding couple's first dance was announced, then the groom danced with his mother, and the bride her father. Then everyone was invited out onto the dance floor.

Knowing he'd keep his promise to her for the rest of the weekend, that keeping that promise was his motivation for wanting to take her out on the dance floor, Ryder stood, held out his hand. "How about it, McKenzie? You up for a foot-stomping two nights in a row?"

Hesitating only a moment, McKenzie placed her hand into his. "I'm not worried. I'll just be sure not to stand next to you during any line dances, and I should be fine."

Perhaps McKenzie had drunk too much of the free-flowing champagne. Perhaps it was how Ryder was putting on such a great show of being enamored with her that even she was convinced.

Perhaps it was how her body melded against his during the slow songs and how their eyes held each other's during fast ones as their bodies moved to the music.

Perhaps it was like he implied and the attraction she felt was simple genetically embedded chemistry that a gorgeous, intelligent man was near and she was DNA coded to respond.

She didn't believe so, but what did she know? She'd gotten things all wrong in her past relationships.

What made her think she'd do any better in a fake one?

Regardless of the reasons why, her body was responding.

To every look, every touch, every whispered comment, every laugh at something she said, every gentle kiss he bestowed on her hair while he held her close and they swayed to Reva's playlist.

Each song was like another round of foreplay, building tension within her, wearing down her reasons why she shouldn't invite Ryder into her bed that night.

It had been a while since she'd had sex.

But she didn't recall ever wanting it quite as badly as she did at the moment.

So badly that she was ready to ditch the wedding, take Ryder home and do all the things to him that her family and friends thought she should already have done.

"What are you thinking?"

McKenzie lifted her gaze to Ryder's. What would he say if she told him she was thinking about how much she'd like to strip his clothes off him and find out if he was as good in bed as she suspected he was?

Would he accuse her of not knowing what she was feeling? Of just being on the rebound and so not capable of rational discernment of her emotions?

"That Reva's wedding went well."

As if he knew that hadn't been what she was thinking, Ryder's brow arched. "Any regrets on coming this weekend?"

"None." She hadn't. Would she say the same if she failed to act on her attraction to Ryder? Would she forever wonder what would have happened if she'd told him she didn't want him to sleep on the floor? That she wanted him in bed, with her, but not to sleep?

Later that night, Kenzie was still wondering the same thing when she finished in the bathroom, came back into her bedroom, and saw Ryder lying on his pallet on the floor.

She paused by the door, hesitant, wondering which she'd regret more: climbing into her bed and falling asleep alone or inviting him into her bed and not sleeping at all?

Having no doubt heard her enter the room and wondering why she'd stopped just inside the door, he opened his eyes.

His beautiful honey-colored eyes that seemed to glow in the soft lamplight.

McKenzie swallowed.

She wanted to have sex with Ryder.

How crazy was that when she knew they weren't really a couple, when she knew that when they returned to Seattle tomorrow evening the pretense would be over and it was all too possible that he'd go back to avoiding her?

They were in the here and now.

In the here and now, Ryder was with her, was lying on her bedroom floor looking at her with those magnificent eyes. It might just be the convenience of proximity that caused the flash of heat, but she saw the lust burning in his gaze that she suspected flickered in her own.

But he didn't say anything, didn't even move, just watched as she crossed the room to stand next to the bed.

He wouldn't say anything, would let her climb into her bed and lie there wishing he was with her.

She couldn't do it.

Her whole life she'd settled when it came to relationships, to sex, to the men in her life.

Tonight, she wasn't settling.

She wanted Ryder, wanted the warmth of his touch, the heat of his kisses, the burn that spread inside her at anticipation of what she was about to do.

Rather than climb into her bed, or even to invite him to join her there, in case he said no, McKenzie knelt, straddled Ryder, her hips positioned perfectly over his as she leaned forward to press her lips to his.

Sexual tension had been building between them all night. All weekend. Longer.

But Ryder hadn't expected McKenzie to act on what was blazing between them.

He'd thought as long as he didn't say anything, she'd get in her bed and go to sleep. Tomorrow they'd go back to Seattle, then he'd make sure their paths didn't cross for long enough for him to get his attraction to her back under control.

Because it was out of control.

Or maybe he'd fallen asleep and was dreaming, and her hair didn't really cascade around him as she explored his mouth with hunger that matched his.

Whatever, he thrust his fingers through the silken tresses and pulled her to him, deepening their kiss.

She shifted above him, and he had to close his eyes to keep from lifting his hips to push into where she straddled his body.

He wanted to strip away their clothes, the thin blanket covering him, and thrust into her for real.

The deeper, the better.

Under different circumstances, he'd roll, pin her beneath him, and take control of what was happening.

He should stop her. Should remind her she was on the rebound. Should remind himself she was on the rebound.

"We should stop. Your emotions are high from the wedding. You'll regret this in the morning," he warned.

"You're wrong," she corrected, shifting her bottom over him. "This has nothing to do with the wedding and everything to do with you. I want this. I want you."

"McKenzie," he groaned. He wanted to do the right thing. For her. For him. He should stop her.

Then again, maybe this was what the entire

weekend had been building up to. What had been building since they'd met.

Whatever the case, Ryder didn't stop her.

Couldn't stop her.

Instead, he used every ounce of willpower to let McKenzie lead, for her to dictate what happened every step of the way, no matter where that took them.

Whatever happened between them would be of her doing, her choice.

He'd wanted her from the beginning. Had only been fooling himself that he was over his fascination with her during the time he'd been avoiding her. He hadn't been over a thing.

Which was why he'd not been able to walk away when she'd needed him to go with her. No way would he have let her spend the weekend with a hired escort.

Perhaps he was no better, but he'd never intentionally hurt her. Had always tried to do the opposite, hence his staying away from her when she'd been with her ex for fear he'd act on his feelings for her, that he'd seduce her into something she didn't want.

He'd been seduced from the moment he'd met her and had instantly wanted her.

Now, she was above him, her hot center pressed over where he ached as she kissed him into oblivious pleasure.

He was oblivious. To all reason. To logic. To common sense. To everything except McKenzie.

When she moved against him, Ryder couldn't keep his hands off her any longer and skimmed them over her back, tracing her spine, cupping her sweet bottom gliding against him.

"Touch me," she moaned. "Please, Ryder, touch me. I need you to."

He planned to touch. Every last inch of her.

Excitement filled him as he slid his hands beneath her T-shirt and pulled the material over her head, revealing her bare chest beneath.

Her bare chest that had him arching upward to wrap his mouth around a pink tip.

Her thighs clenched at his waist as he gave a gentle suck, then he moved to the matching peak.

She leaned forward, supporting her upper half by placing a hand to each side of his head, giving him easy access to the treasures he'd uncovered.

He suckled, teased, licked and nipped until, moaning, she arched, then sat up enough to support her weight on her knees to each side of his hips. Her hands tugged on his T-shirt. Ryder raised his upper half from the floor, making removal of his shirt easier.

"You have a beautiful body," she praised, running her hands over his shoulders, then down his chest to mere inches away from where her lower half met his.

"As do you," he assured her, reaching for her breasts again. "As do you."

They kissed, touched, grinded against each other, until both were desperate for remaining clothing barriers to be gone.

McKenzie moved off him, and he helped strip away her pajama shorts and underwear.

When he reached for the waistband of his pajama bottoms, she covered his hand with hers.

Please don't stop me, he thought, at the same time as he had no doubt he'd do just that if it was what she said she wanted.

"I don't have protection," she said instead, disappointment shining in her eyes.

Relief filled him.

"I do. In my wallet."

Mixed emotions crossed her face. "Of course, you do."

He paused in reaching for where he'd left his wallet on her nightstand. "Did you want me to say I didn't have protection? We don't have to do this if it's not what you want," he reminded her.

They shouldn't do this. Deep down he knew that. He also knew it would take a stronger man than him to deny McKenzie if she wanted to make love with him.

"I do want this, so very much, only…" She closed her eyes. "It makes sense you'd have protection. I'm glad you have protection, and yet…

well, I guess it makes me aware of how much more experienced you are than me."

Ryder snorted with a bit of irony. Once upon a time he'd had an active sex life, but not since moving to Seattle. Quite the opposite. Sex for the sake of sex had quit appealing years before.

"It might surprise you how long it's been since I've had sex."

For months, he'd wanted only one woman and she'd belonged to another man.

Tonight, she belonged to him.

Her body.

Her mind.

Her heart?

Self-conscious that she was naked and had stopped him prior to his removing his pajama bottoms, McKenzie nodded, although she wasn't sure if she was agreeing with his comment that how long it had been since he'd had sex would surprise her or if she was nodding her agreement with the thought that he should be naked, too.

Had it really been that long for him?

Did it matter? She wanted him. He wanted her—for the moment, at least.

For now, that was enough.

Rather than say anything more, she finished the job he'd started, pulling his pajama bottoms and underwear off in one movement with the help of his lifting his hips.

Her breath caught at the true magnificence of his body. She visually traced down his shoulders, his chiseled chest, down his abs to where a trail of hair pointed to pleasure. Just wow.

Her gaze lifted to his. "You're sure you're really a heart surgeon and not a professional athlete?"

She'd thought he looked the part of a television doctor in the past. Seeing him naked reinforced her thoughts that his body was made to be admired.

She admired. Oh, how she admired.

His brow lifted. "Who better to take care of their body than someone educated on the benefits of exercise and proper diet?"

"True." Not that McKenzie hadn't enjoyed every bite of the cake and goodies served at the wedding—she had. "But I don't know of any real-life doctor who looks like you."

"I'm not the only one who works out."

"You're the only one who makes my fingers want to do this." She traced her finger over his chest, down his abs and happy trail in the pattern her eyes had previously taken.

Ryder sucked in air, his stomach muscles tightening. McKenzie thrilled at his reaction to her touch, that there was no denying that he wanted her.

Yet when she went to touch him where he

strained toward her, he grabbed her hand, stopping her.

"Not yet. If you touch me there, I'll have to have you soon thereafter."

McKenzie's thighs clenched at the prospect, her whole body tingling. "Isn't that the idea?"

He shook his head. "My idea is to touch and kiss every inch of you first."

His words set off explosions in her head, in the pit of her belly, at her very core. She always had thought him a smart man. They'd go with his idea. Most definitely. Because she wanted him touching her, kissing her.

Every inch of her wanted to be claimed by him.

"Oh. Okay."

"Yeah, oh. Okay." His words were half-teasing, but his eyes glittered in ways she'd never seen him look at her. In ways she'd never seen any man look at her.

Pure male power and possessiveness. She was his and he planned to claim his prize. Her.

McKenzie saw stars. Lots and lots of stars.

Which was pretty amazing since she lay on her bedroom floor, gasping for air, basking in the glow of having had really great sex, the best sex of her life.

The best sex of anyone's life.

Had to be.

And that was with them trying to keep quiet so as not to wake anyone else in the house.

McKenzie had wanted to scream out in pleasure several times, and almost had with her last orgasm, but Ryder had caught her cry with his mouth as he'd toppled over the edge with her.

The man was incredible.

Pure and simple.

His intelligence, his kindness, his body that moved with hers in a primal rhythm she'd never danced before, one of pure, orgasmic pleasure.

She'd done a better job with picking out a fake boyfriend than she ever had picking out a real one.

"That was better than I thought it would be."

McKenzie's happy haze dissipated. Still breathing hard, her heart hammering against her ribcage, she rolled over to look at him. "Did you think I'd be bad?"

Chuckling, he rolled onto his side, too, and faced her. "I thought you'd be wonderful, and you were. More so than I'd thought possible."

"Nice save."

"The truth." He cupped her face. "You were there. There was nothing mediocre about what we just shared."

"You're very good," she admitted.

"As are you."

He'd certainly made her feel good, made her feel sexy, as if he'd read and aced the manual to her body because he knew every trick to eliciting a response.

And, although she was still breathless from what they'd just done, she put her hand against his chest, felt his heart, still beating as erratically as hers, and took comfort that she wasn't alone in what she'd just experienced.

And because she could, she leaned over and kissed where she'd touched.

"McKenzie, I don't think you should—"

"Shh…" she whispered. "I know it's too soon. That's okay. I just want to touch you. Slower this time."

Because she wanted to make as many memories as possible before the sun rose and their time in Tennessee ended.

As with the previous morning, Ryder beat her out of bed. Literally bed for them both as at some point during the night, they'd moved from his pallet to her bed and she'd slept next to him.

Not necessarily cuddled against him, but his arm had been around her when she'd dozed off into exhausted, but happy sleep.

She'd missed that arm when she'd awakened, missed the man she'd hoped to wake next to and even, perhaps, kiss good morning, too.

She supposed it was no wonder she'd slept late. There hadn't been a lot of sleeping going on during the night and she suspected it had been almost morning when they'd moved to her bed.

That she'd enjoyed the night so much frightened her. She was just out of her relationship with Paul less than a month ago. She'd asked Ryder to come with her because she hadn't wanted to jump into a new relationship and had never dreamed she'd become so emotionally entangled with him.

Had never dreamed they'd have done the things they'd done last night.

She needed to be careful. Ryder was a great guy, a phenomenal lover, but that didn't mean he'd want anything more than this weekend with her.

Did she want more than this weekend?

That hadn't been her goal when inviting Ryder. Quite the opposite. She'd planned to return to Seattle, take time to enjoy the city, enjoy life and her amazing career, to take some time for herself, no boyfriend required.

Which left her where this morning?

McKenzie wanted coffee but opted for a shower and full face of makeup prior to making her way to the kitchen.

"Morning," her mother, Mark and her cousin's family greeted.

But McKenzie's eyes zeroed in on one person. One person who had mumbled a good morning, too, but who had barely glanced her way. Was he as confused about how they should act this morning as she was? Trying to figure out what last night had meant? Or if it had meant anything at all other than that they were physically compatible?

Very physically compatible.

How did one act the morning after the most amazing sex of her life which just happened to be with a pretend boyfriend and her family was there to watch her every move?

No wonder he couldn't look at her.

"You slept late this morning."

Leave it to her brother to point that out.

"I'm still on Seattle time." True, although it had nothing to do with her being the last one to rise.

"I can't believe you're already leaving," her mother sighed. "I don't want you to go."

"Me, either," she admitted. "But I love my life in Seattle." She really did. "You should come visit."

"I will," her brother commented and was the only one to do so.

McKenzie understood that. She was petrified of flying but forced herself to do so on occasion. Roberta hadn't flown since her husband died. McKenzie doubted her mother ever would, again.

She walked over to her mother, kissed the top of her head. "I'll come home again soon, Mama. Maybe at Christmas if I can arrange my schedule to be off work for a few days."

"That would be wonderful." Her mother patted McKenzie's arm, then reached out and placed her hand over Ryder's forearm and did the same. "You're invited, too, of course."

Ryder, who'd been watching the interplay while still avoiding making eye contact with McKenzie, gave her mom a half-smile. "Thanks. I'd like that. I've enjoyed my first visit."

His only visit? How crazy that his doing what she wanted, pretending to be her boyfriend, left her unable to know how to take anything he did or said when her family was around. Would he really like to come back or had he just said that?

Ugh. McKenzie's brain hurt. She had no one to blame but herself. But the smiles on everyone's faces all weekend, the lack of worrying about how heartbroken she'd been when she moved to Seattle and no new worries over Paul having done the same just over a month ago had been worth it.

Odd, it seemed a lifetime ago since she'd been involved with Paul, planning to spend the rest of her life with him, and yet it really hadn't been that long ago.

McKenzie got her coffee, joined the others at the table, and pretended that she wasn't hyper-aware of Ryder being next to her.

She'd not had awkward mornings-after with Clay or Paul. At least, not that she recalled. Then again, she'd not had incredible nights with them, either. Just… She glanced toward Ryder, willing him to look up and smile at her, anything, just some sign that things were going to be okay. That when this was all said and done, they'd at least be friends.

McKenzie never got her smile.

The morning passed quickly with lots of family stopping by to say their goodbyes.

No one commented on the tension between her and Ryder. It seemed impossible that they couldn't have picked up on it, and she wondered if they knew what they'd been up to during the night.

They'd kept the noise down. At least, she thought so. The reality was, she'd been so caught up in Ryder, she really didn't know how much noise they'd made.

Regardless of what her family knew or didn't know, they'd given lots of heartfelt goodbyes, well-wishes and pleas to come visit again soon.

McKenzie would.

Hopefully she'd make it home at Christmas or the week after Christmas.

By the time they were in the rental van on their way toward Nashville Airport, McKenzie was an emotional mess. From saying goodbye to her family, to knowing she was about to board a plane, to not knowing how Ryder really felt about what had happened between them.

She gripped the steering wheel tighter than necessary, cast a glance toward where he fiddled with his phone.

"Thank you for coming with me, Ryder."

He looked her way. "Sure thing."

"My family loved you. The trip couldn't have been any more wonderful. I really do owe you."

"I'm glad it all worked out."

Maybe they would have progressed to beyond pleasantries, but Ryder's phone rang.

McKenzie could tell the call was from someone at the hospital. When that call finished, he made another, checking on a patient. Was he purposely avoiding talking with her?

Was he worried she'd read too much into the night before? Afraid she was going to expect more from him?

Did he not realize the thought of diving into another relationship scared her almost as much as flying?

She sighed.

He'd given her what he'd agreed to, gone above and beyond. What had she expected? For him to date her a few years, then dump her?

Much better if they had their one night and left it at that.

Only the thought that they'd go back to how things were before didn't feel right. She didn't want that. She wanted… She didn't know what she wanted, but not for them to go back to completely avoiding each other.

They had an hour to kill at the airport, found seats near their terminal, but were surrounded by other passengers waiting on their flight, precluding any real conversation.

Ryder wandered off, came back with a book, and started reading.

Yep. That was a sure sign he didn't plan on them talking on the plane. Maybe he thought there was nothing more to say and wasn't suffering from the same mental tug-of-war that she was. And not just the one with flying anxiety and logic that she'd be fine.

Ugh. She dug into her bag, pulled out a prescription bottle and took her anxiolytic tablet. Maybe she wouldn't fall asleep on him this time. If she did, well, at least she wouldn't have to sit in five hours of uneasy silence.

If she made it through the flight.

She'd done so well up to this point, not having a single panic attack while checking into the airport. Possibly because she was so distracted by the man next to her.

Think happy thoughts, she told herself over and over.

Unfortunately, her most recent happy thoughts all seemed to star Ryder.

After they boarded the plane, got settled into their seats, Ryder turned to her, his gaze full of concern. "You doing okay?"

Emotions hitting her that he'd finally looked at her, really looked at her, that his eyes revealed he wasn't indifferent, she nodded. "I think so."

"Good."

But when the plane started moving, making its way toward the runway, McKenzie changed her mind, wondering if she was going to come out of her skin.

Breathing was difficult. Sweating not so much so.

Don't do this, she ordered herself. She was fine. This was ridiculous.

Only sitting in the seat was becoming more and more challenging.

"You got this," Ryder assured her, taking her hand. "Just take a deep breath and let it out slowly. You can do this."

It was the first he'd touched her since they'd fallen asleep next to each other after a whole lot of touching and she almost cried out at the burn of his skin against hers.

McKenzie's poor nervous system must have been on overload at the onslaught of sensations holding his hand added to her already hyped-up, under-attack neurons.

She stared at their entwined hands, tried to form words to ask him where they went from this weekend. That conversation would distract her from where she was, that she was about to fly.

Then again, his answers could trigger anxiety of its own.

The thought of not seeing him, spending time with him, hurt, but the thought of continuing what they'd started would cause pain unlike any she'd ever known.

"Your family is great, McKenzie."

She knew what he was doing and appreciated his wanting to help her through the next few minutes. Then again, he could just want to save himself a whole lot of embarrassment if she gave in to her desire to claw her way out of the plane.

"I liked them."

"They liked you, too." Understatement of the century. "Nothing would please my mother more than if you were my real boyfriend."

Ack. Had she really just said that? What was she trying to do? Pour gasoline on the fire and see just how hot her anxiety could burn?

McKenzie glanced up just in time to see Ryder's dark eyes. She really should have just kept her mouth shut the entire flight home. Maybe that would be best for the rest of the flight before she said all kinds of other crazy things.

Things like that because of him what could have been the worst weekend of her life had actually been one of the best.

Things like that last night had exceeded anything she'd ever known and had set the bar so high that the thought of never reaching that pinnacle again was almost enough to make her cry.

Things like that if she didn't know she'd only end up dumped down the road, she might want to pursue a real relationship with him.

But she did know. History had taught her well.

The pilot announced for the crew to prepare for takeoff. McKenzie automatically dug her fingers into her seat and braced herself.

She very seriously doubted that Ryder planned to kiss her through today's takeoff.

No doubt he was eager to be back in Seattle, away from her and their pretend relationship.

Last night hadn't been pretend.

Don't be silly, McKenzie, she scolded herself.

Last night had been nothing more than sex. Good sex. Amazing, blow-her-mind sex. But sex was probably always that way for Ryder.

As the plane taxied down the runway, McKenzie's stomach tightened, as did her grip. Ryder must have felt sorry for her, because he squeezed her hand.

She focused on where his hand covered hers and remarkably, her rising panic waned some. It didn't disappear, but did ease enough that she settled back, closed her eyes, and let the events of the past weekend play out through her mind.

No matter what, she was glad Ryder had come to Tennessee with her, that she'd come home to be in Reva's wedding and to visit with her family.

Her only regret was that she'd waited until her last night in Tennessee to have sex with Ryder.

With that thought, she squeezed her eyes shut, gritted her teeth, and forced each breath in and out as the plane sped up and lifted off the ground.

There had been no kiss this time.

Nor were there any false hopes regarding anything between them being real.

CHAPTER TWELVE

R<small>YDER SLUNG</small> M<small>C</small>K<small>ENZIE</small>'<small>S</small> bag strap over his shoulder, along with his own. "That it?"

Releasing the handle on her suitcase that he'd gotten off the baggage carousel, she nodded. "Yes, thank you. I can carry that, so you don't have to."

"Not a problem. I've got it." Mostly because he wanted to walk her to her car.

Hell, he wanted to bring her to his apartment and make love to her in the privacy of his bed.

But he wouldn't.

Whether she'd had sex with him out of an emotional post-wedding high, or just because he'd been convenient, or just that she'd decided to act on the physical chemistry between them, the reality was, less than a month ago she'd planned to spend her life with another man.

He'd learned his lesson well enough in the past and wouldn't be making that mistake again. He might have been her pretend boyfriend, but he wouldn't be McKenzie's rebound guy.

He should have stopped her the night before, because he could no longer look at her without having flashbacks of her above him, moving sensuously and rocking his world.

Yes, he'd always felt desire when he saw her. But now he knew—knew and wanted more.

Only he didn't.

He and McKenzie had had a great weekend together. A weekend that was so much more than he'd ever expected to have with her. It was enough.

It had to be.

He wouldn't have McKenzie be the next Anna in his life.

They reached her car and he loaded the luggage into the trunk, then turned to face her.

"Um, thanks for going with me." She toyed with her key fob. "For everything, really."

"You're welcome."

"I…um…well, I guess I'll be going." She turned to get into the car, then paused, turned back to him, stood on her tiptoes and pressed a quick kiss to the corner of his mouth. "I'm not sure why you agreed to this weekend, Ryder, but you certainly saved me a lot of heartache. Thank you."

He hoped he hadn't caused a lot of heartache for himself in the process.

"You're welcome." How banal.

She eyed him a bit nervously. "So, where do we go from here?"

He stared into her green eyes and wondered

what it was she wanted him to say. "A real relationship between us wouldn't work."

Statistics said they'd fail. Rebound relationships rarely even made it beyond the six months' mark.

She gave him a wry smile, as if she'd known that was what he'd say and didn't disagree. "I'll admit our pretend relationship was pretty fab, though."

True. It had been. Enough so that the thought of not seeing her, not holding her or kissing her again seemed impossible.

"So." She let out an exaggerated breath. "Is this where we just walk away and go back to the way things were?"

"Yes." It's what they should do.

"Do you really think we can do that? After, well, you know?" she asked, still fiddling with her key fob.

"No, I guess not."

"Me, either." She seemed relieved at his answer. "But I hope we can still be friends. I really do appreciate everything you did." She hesitated, as if she considered saying more.

He didn't want her gratitude.

What he wanted... Hell, if he knew.

He'd be grateful he had this weekend to know her better, to get such an up-close glimpse at the woman who'd captured his imagination. A pretend weekend relationship would be enough.

"Goodbye, McKenzie."

Her eyes widened a bit in shock, then she nodded, mumbled a goodbye of her own.

Just as he started to lean down to kiss the corner of her mouth, she stuck out her hand. His gaze dropped to it.

All pretense was gone. They were back to reality. It's what he'd crazily agreed to, what she'd always wanted.

Ryder shook her hand, wondering if that would be the last time they'd ever touch.

Wondering what she'd do if he pulled her close and kissed her.

Which would be stupid since he knew this was goodbye.

She pulled her hand free, searched his eyes for a brief second, then climbed into her car.

Rather than head toward where he'd parked, Ryder watched McKenzie drive away, wondering at how he could already miss her when she'd never really been his to miss.

Ryder was back to avoiding her.

Three weeks had passed since their trip to Tennessee. McKenzie shouldn't care that she knew he put effort into making sure their paths crossed as little as possible.

She should appreciate his efforts as it prevented awkward encounters and second thoughts

on whether she should have let him walk away
so easily.

Nothing about being away from him felt easy
and she didn't appreciate his avoidance.

Like now. She'd been on call at the hospital all
night, had just gotten paged to check on a neonate
in the NICU, and there he'd been, larger than life,
and making her heart pound so hard it had to be
creating shockwaves on the plethora of cardiac
monitors in the unit.

When she'd spotted him her smile had been
automatic. Even the tiniest glimpse of him made
her insides light up. But that light had dimmed
almost as fast as it appeared. As rather than return her smile, he'd given a nod of acknowledg-
ment, then turned away.

Which hurt.

How could he just turn away as if they hadn't
had the most amazing sex on her bedroom floor,
twice, before climbing up into her bed and holding each other long into the night?

As if they hadn't shared looks and kisses an
entire weekend?

As if... Ugh. She had to stop.

Ryder had done her a favor. Had pretended to
be her boyfriend. He'd never promised, or even
alluded to wanting, anything more.

Anything more scared her. One weekend as
Ryder's pretend girlfriend had turned her world

upside down. What if they got involved for real, how would she cope when he walked away?

Clay and Paul's walking away had hurt, but she'd survived. With the impact Ryder had had on her psyche, she wasn't so sure she could handle being dumped by him.

Which was enough to keep her from reaching out to him and telling him how much she missed him.

McKenzie's phone buzzed from her scrub pocket. She glanced at the message and her heart squeezed for more than one reason.

Whether either of them wanted to or not, she and Ryder would soon be forced to interact.

Sawyer Little was in respiratory distress and on her way to the hospital via ambulance.

McKenzie met the paramedics wheeling Sawyer into the emergency department. She'd wanted to be right there when the baby arrived.

As had Ryder.

Working beside him added a new level to the intensity of the moment, to the stress of Sawyer's heart possibly failing.

Testing immediately began.

Nurses carried out orders as McKenzie and Ryder gave them.

"Please don't let her be in heart failure," McKenzie whispered softly as she ran the ultrasound conducer over the baby's chest. "Please. Please. Please."

The surgical sites looked good. The rebuilt aorta had good blood flow via the surgically connected proximal pulmonary artery. The pulmonary veins had increased pressure, which happened sometimes, but that shouldn't have put the baby into respiratory distress. However, the fluid built up in the baby's lungs could, and had.

Pneumonia? Or her heart's inability to efficiently pump fluid and the fluid had backed up into Sawyer's lungs, filling the tiny air sacs and preventing oxygen exchange?

Sawyer needed to go back on life support stat to take the workload off her heart and clear out the fluid, if it was cardiac in nature.

If infectious in nature, well, they'd deal with that, too.

"The surgical site looks patent," Ryder commented. "Her blood is being oxygenated. I don't see any evidence of a clot or failure of the repairs."

McKenzie agreed. "It's possibly pneumonia."

Ryder nodded. "I hope not, but not uncommon after being on a ventilator for several days. It could have been slowly worsening since her hospital discharge."

McKenzie ordered blood cultures and labs, determined to quickly get to the root of whatever was causing Sawyer's problems.

The baby's life depended on it.

"I'm going to suction her," Ryder said.

They continued to examine the baby, working, prodding and poking.

Tubes seemed to be coming from every aspect of the baby's body.

"I still don't find any evidence of a clot, but her rhythm is jumpy."

"I'm ordering an inotropic," she told him, then did so.

Ryder glanced toward a nurse and gave a verbal order for additional medications.

"Ryder!" McKenzie couldn't hold her cry in when Sawyer's rhythm took a drastic drop.

But he was already responding, giving the baby a nudge.

Knowing time was of the essence, McKenzie pushed medication into the IV port, then got her intubated.

McKenzie and Ryder stayed with the baby over the next two hours, working with her almost nonstop to insure the tiny heart didn't succumb to the strain of the excess fluid and ensuing shock.

Once the baby was stable, they transferred her to the neonatal intensive care unit. Kenzie and Ryder stayed close during the transfer.

"I can stay with her," Ryder offered as they headed toward the unit.

McKenzie shot him an *Are you crazy?* look. "I'm not leaving, if that's what you're getting at."

"You've been here all night."

He knew her on-call schedule? She supposed knowing would make it easier for him to avoid coming around.

"I'm fine." Mostly, she was. She'd caught a few hours' sleep here and there during the long night.

"I'll be here, anyway, McKenzie. It seems crazy for you to stay past your on-call time when I know you're tired."

Don't read anything into his concern. It wasn't personal. He was just being nice.

Perhaps she was tired, or just cranky, but she didn't want his nice.

Her chin lifted. "I'm staying."

Ryder's gaze narrowed and he studied her, then seemed to accept he couldn't change her mind. "I get that, just hate that you're doing so unnecessarily."

She frowned. "And I get that you'd rather I not stay so you don't have to be around me, but tough luck. Sawyer is my patient, and I'm staying."

At her comment, Ryder winced ever so slightly, but didn't deny her claim.

There wasn't a need when they both knew what she said was true.

Too bad being here with him, even under duress and when she really should be feeling tired, had her feeling more alive than she'd been in… three weeks.

* * *

McKenzie should have gone home, Ryder thought for the dozenth time. Why had she had to be so stubborn? What had she been trying to prove?

Instead, she'd set up watch in Sawyer's bay, determined to be close if anything changed on the baby's status while they waited on test results.

Once Sawyer was settled into the NICU bay and her heart rhythm and oxygen saturation, lower than normal even with supplementation and breathing assistance, stabilized, Ryder had gone to check on another patient, the patient he'd actually come to the hospital to check, but had gotten side-tracked from by Sawyer's arrival.

Coming back to the infant's bay, he'd not been surprised to find McKenzie in a chair, half-asleep, but ready to jump into action at the first sounding of a vital sign change alarm.

She didn't open her eyes at his entering the room, but her breathing pattern changed, so he knew she wasn't asleep.

She knew he was there and was choosing not to have to interact with him. Her accusation earlier hit him. He did avoid her. How could he not when being near her made him want to forget common sense and lessons hard learned?

Surely, she agreed avoidance was for the best or she wouldn't be pretending to be asleep.

He checked Sawyer, eyeing every one of the dozen monitors keeping tabs on the baby.

Just as he was turning to leave the bay, McKenzie's phone went off. When she answered, he could tell it was the lab.

He waited, wanting to know what the test results were.

When she hung up the phone, she turned her lovely, concern-filled green eyes his way.

"Sawyer's white blood cell count is twenty-seven thousand."

Ryder winced. Her numbers should be under ten thousand.

"The fluid is from pneumonia," he said unnecessarily.

McKenzie nodded. "The lab is sending off the sputum sample you suctioned, but it'll be a few days before we know for sure. I'm ordering additional RNA viral testing, then I'll go talk to Sawyer's parents."

"I'll stay here while you're with them."

She started to argue. He could see the denial on the tip of her tongue, but she stopped herself, nodding instead. "I plan to okay the Littles to come back here with her for a while, to give them some time with her."

She didn't say *just in case*, but he heard the unspoken words.

"They'll appreciate the time with her."

McKenzie nodded, glancing toward the baby with so many wires and tubes attached that she seemed almost unreal.

"They have to be terrified that she's in distress," McKenzie said, so softly Ryder barely heard her.

Ryder imagined any parent would be. Even without the current situation, Sawyer's parents had a long, stressful road ahead of them due to the baby's congenital heart defects and any number of complications that could occur.

That likely would occur from time to time.

McKenzie knew that, but her heartfelt whisper didn't surprise him. McKenzie had a big heart, one that loved her job and her patients.

His reaching for her hand was automatic. He regretted it the moment her surprised gaze jerked to his.

The moment her cool-to-the-touch skin still managed to shoot fire to his core that spread through his whole being, reminding him of how it had been with McKenzie.

How he'd been with her.

"Ryder, I…" She paused, pulled her hand away. "I've got to go speak with Sawyer's parents."

With that, McKenzie left, but it wasn't long until she returned to the bay with the Littles. Ryder's heart went out to the young couple who couldn't take their eyes off their baby and all the attached tubes and wires. They'd seen worse after her heart repair, but no doubt the image was still intimidating.

"Let's give them a few minutes," he suggested,

taking McKenzie's elbow, ignoring that he was yet again touching her, and guiding her from the bay. There were several nurses at the nurses' station, and Ryder just kept walking.

See why he couldn't be near her? His hand was still on her elbow.

When they reached the elevator, Kenzie pulled her elbow from his grasp. "Where are we going?"

"To the cafeteria. When's the last time you ate something?"

She gave him a blank look.

"That's what I thought. Even though it's essentially a waiting game to see if Sawyer responds to the medication we're giving her, I imagine you're planning to stay close tonight."

McKenzie nodded.

"Let's get something in you so you don't get run down and end up picking up a bug yourself."

For a moment he thought she was going to tell him that whether or not she got run down wasn't any of his business, but instead, she sighed. "I wouldn't mind a cup of coffee."

Despite the tension between them, he couldn't help grinning.

"What?"

"You and your coffee."

"Just because you don't like it doesn't mean it's not amazing stuff."

"Apparently."

When they arrived at the mostly empty hospital cafeteria, they went through the line, each purchasing a few items before they sat down at a table together.

"How is your family?"

"Good. They've asked about you."

Ryder looked at her in surprise. Not that her family had asked about him, but that she was telling him.

"I told Mark the truth. He was livid I'd felt the need to bring a pretend boyfriend home, but admitted he also understood why I had, and, on second thought, he thought it brilliant."

"Your brother is a good guy." He'd truly liked the pilot.

"Most days." McKenzie sighed. "He said the same thing about you."

"That I was a good guy?"

Pulling the top off a yogurt cup, she nodded. "He said you had to be a good guy to agree to be my pretend boyfriend."

"It wasn't so bad."

"But not that good, either?"

Ryder met her gaze. Was she talking sex? Because she'd been there, knew sex between them had been beyond good.

She glanced down. "Sorry. I shouldn't have asked that."

Let it go, he ordered himself, but couldn't. "I'm curious. Why shouldn't you have asked?"

She took a deep breath. "Because, in spite of

everything that happened, you're back to avoiding me."

There was that. That she sounded hurt gutted him. He didn't want to hurt her. Not ever.

"Things are complicated," he admitted, searching for the right words and not sure it was possible to find them.

"If we hadn't had sex, would you feel differently?"

Sex with McKenzie had been life-altering, but it wasn't the sex he missed most. Yes, he wanted her, to kiss her and make love to her sweet body over and over.

But it was her smile, her wit, the way when her gaze met his he knew what she was thinking, the way when she laughed his insides filled with joy, that he missed most.

Which made him a fool. He'd have sworn he'd learned his lesson with Anna and would never let his emotions get caught in a rebound relationship again.

How wrong he'd been.

"No, McKenzie," he admitted, giving a humorless snort at the irony of the situation. Had he really thought he could be her pretend boyfriend without ramifications? "If we'd not had sex, I'd feel the same."

Which was the unfortunate truth.

CHAPTER THIRTEEN

McKenzie stayed at the hospital that night.

Sawyer remained stable on life support but showed no sign of improvement. They were keeping her lightly sedated to decrease tissue oxygen demand and to make tolerating the ventilation easier, so the baby hadn't regained consciousness.

Not that she necessarily would have anyway.

Sawyer's parents had also stayed at the hospital all night. McKenzie liked the couple, watched them a bit enviously as they comforted each other at the depth of their daughter's illness.

Had Ryder's parents once sat in a hospital room watching over their ill daughter, knowing only a miracle would keep them from losing her? A miracle that hadn't come.

No. No. No. She wasn't going to think of him.

Nothing about the man made sense.

She just needed to stay away from him.

She was on her way out to the parking garage when her phone dinged. For one crazy moment she wondered if it was Ryder. If he'd had second thoughts and realized sex between them had changed everything.

You're crazy, girl. Sex doesn't change things for guys. Not outside romantic movies.

Besides, she didn't want to be hurt again. Three strikes and you were out, right? Clay and Paul had already done their numbers on her heart. She wouldn't give Ryder the chance.

Once inside her car, she pulled out her phone, expecting to see a message from the hospital or even Reva as they'd texted and called several times.

What she hadn't expected was to see a text from Paul.

"I've missed you."

Hello. McKenzie's eyes widened at Paul's admission. She took a sip of her wine because she didn't know what to say.

What she couldn't say was that she'd missed him.

Ryder on the other hand…nope, she wasn't going there.

"I was hoping you'd say you'd missed me too," he said, giving a nervous laugh. "Maybe just a little?"

McKenzie was saved by the waiter bringing their meals and her making a pretense of being starved as she dug into her sweet potato.

McKenzie wrapped her lips around her fork and eyed her ex. He truly was a handsome man. A good man.

But her heart didn't do somersaults when she looked at him.

Not like… Ugh, there she went again.

"I made a mistake, McKenzie. I'm not sure what I was thinking breaking things off. I think I just hoped our being apart for a while would make you ready for us to begin the next phase of our lives."

That got her attention.

"What next phase of our lives?"

"Marriage, kids, you know."

"That's a cop-out, Paul. We'd discussed marriage."

"Always in the terms of way off in the future. I'd been trying to pin you down on wedding plans for months and you kept putting me off."

She didn't recall any major discussions about getting married, just vague ones about someday. She'd been good with someday as she'd not been ready to slow down on her workload.

"There was no rush," she admitted.

"Don't you think there should have been? That you should have been excited about being my wife?"

McKenzie opened her mouth to deny his claim. She had been…or had she?

She'd started dating Paul after her mother's signing her up for that speed dating event. Had she fallen into their relationship for convenience?

Continued seeing him because he was a good man—comfortable?

"You never let yourself fully get onboard with our relationship, and I always felt it," he continued. "I always wondered if it was that other guy, the one before me, but I can't help but wonder if he didn't run into the same wall I did. That you refuse to let yourself love."

That was a joke. She loved. She'd loved Clay. She'd loved Paul. She'd loved Ryder. They'd all been the ones to leave.

She'd loved Ryder? That one had her pausing. She hadn't loved Ryder. She'd...

Her gaze met Paul's.

A whole lot of realizations swamped her. Realizations that she had cared deeply for Clay, for the man sitting across from her, but she hadn't been in love with either.

But she had been in love.

Was in love.

With a man as emotionally inaccessible as... as she'd been to the man she was dining with.

And yet...

"I—I'm sorry, Paul." She folded her napkin. "You're a good man, but if tonight is about us getting back together, it's not going to happen."

Just being content, comfortable in a relationship, was overrated, and not something she'd ever settle for again.

* * *

McKenzie strolled through Pike Place Market, stopping at one vendor's booth, then another, pausing to watch workers toss a purchased fish, then meandering over to her favorite coffee shop to buy a cup of pick-me-up.

Coffee soon finished, she stopped at a booth, bought a gorgeous bouquet.

It was only a few short blocks to her condo, but rather than go straight home, McKenzie headed down to the pier, traveling past a couple of cruise ships as she headed in the direction of the aquarium. She enjoyed each step, breathing in the seaside air, embracing the wind against her face.

She truly loved this city. Eventually, it was possible she'd move back to Nashville, but other than her family being so far away, her life was in Seattle.

McKenzie paused when she came to the pier, walked out onto the decking, and wondered if she'd see any seals.

Leaning against the railing, she watched a fishing boat in the distance, listened to seagulls calling, the sounds of the city behind her, sounds of the harbor before her.

Having the day off work was nice but meant zero chance of bumping into Ryder.

She closed her eyes, breathed in the sea air.

She planned to talk to him. To tell him everything in her heart.

Ryder was worth taking a chance that he'd tell her he didn't want a relationship. Worth risking having her heart shattered down the line if he was willing to give them a chance.

Ryder was worth facing her fears, worth risking heartbreak, worth being dumped a third time.

McKenzie's heartbeat sped up and she gripped her bouquet tighter as she stared out over the water.

Was Ryder at the hospital? Home? Somewhere else?

He didn't live that far away. She could walk the few blocks but seeing him was too imperative to go on a wild goose chase.

Taking her phone from her pocket, she dialed his number.

When he answered, her heart soared.

"You've heard the good news?"

The good news was that he'd answered his phone. Hearing his voice set endorphins off that had her smiling despite how nervous she was to have called him.

"Sawyer's white blood cell count is nine thousand." Excitement filled his voice at the baby's normal lab value. "I took her off the vent and she's holding her own."

"Oh, wow!" she said, getting distracted by what he'd said. "That is good news." All her patients were special, but Sawyer was more so, probably because of the connection with Ryder. "You're at the hospital?"

"I was until about an hour ago," he told her. "I came home to grab a shower and something to eat. I'll probably head back that way later this evening."

He was home.

McKenzie began walking in the direction of his apartment.

"That's great about Sawyer," she said, clutching her flowers in one hand and her phone to her ear with the other. "I know the Littles must be ecstatic."

"They are. Hopefully, if Sawyer continues to improve, she can go home in a few days."

"I'll swing by to check on her when I'm at the hospital tomorrow, and to say hi to the Littles."

"Sounds good." Silence then. "Is everything okay?"

"I've been at Pike Place," she told him, not wanting him to end the call. Not when hearing his voice motivated her feet to move faster. "For once, there's not a cloud in sight and the sunshine is absolutely gorgeous. I'd say, everything is wonderful."

At least, she hoped it would soon be.

A little confused by McKenzie's call, Ryder hung up his phone and put it on his bathroom counter.

She'd caught him just after he'd gotten out of

the shower. He'd been standing there, towel-dried hair, towel around waist, talking to her as if they were old friends.

He blamed his excitement over Sawyer's improvement.

But he could just as easily have blamed his excitement on hearing McKenzie's voice.

Ryder finished drying off, went to his bedroom and pulled out a pair of sweats to go for a run.

Running cleared his head.

After talking with McKenzie, his head needed clearing. He missed her.

Despite his still damp hair, he pulled a T-shirt over his head, then grabbed socks and shoes.

Just as he was tying his tennis shoes, his door buzzer rang.

"It's me, McKenzie."

Ryder's hands shook. McKenzie was outside his apartment building, wanting to be let inside.

"That's not a good idea."

"Ryder, I'm not going anywhere until we talk. Let me in."

"By the hair on your chinny-chin-chin?" Because her threatening to huff and puff and blow away his best intentions wouldn't surprise him. She had the power.

"There's no hair on my chin," she countered, sounding so indignant he grinned in spite of his inner turmoil.

"The code is seven, seven, six, seven." Immediately, he regretted giving her access to get into the building.

They didn't need to be in his apartment. Alone. He couldn't be trusted to keep a straight mind.

Only when she knocked and he opened the door, meaning to go outside the apartment and suggest they go for a walk, she smiled so brilliantly at him he forgot everything, including how to breathe.

"Hello, Ryder," she said as she stepped around him and into his living area. "Nice place."

Closing his apartment door, he turned, blinked at where she was taking in his home. "What are you doing here?"

She gave a lopsided smile. "I'd think that obvious. I came to talk to you."

"We just talked on the phone." Noticing what she was holding, his forehead scrunched. "Nice flowers. Are they for me?"

She glanced down at the multicolored bouquet, then laughed. "That would be fitting under the circumstances. Here."

She held them out toward him, but Ryder didn't move to take them. "What circumstances? Why are you at my apartment, McKenzie?"

"You aren't going to make this easy, are you?" She took a deep breath. "Ryder Andrews, I'm crazy about you, miss you like mad and am here to ask you an important question."

She really had gone mad.

"Will you be my boyfriend this weekend? Only, this time, for real?"

Okay, so not what McKenzie had planned. At all. She'd thought she had everything straight on what she'd say, but then she'd seen him, and all she'd really wanted to do was throw her arms around him and tell him how much she'd missed him.

"McKenzie," he began, looking torn. "You know how I feel."

"Actually, I don't know how you feel," she interrupted, waving the flowers at him. "What I know is that because you got hurt in your relationship with Anna, you're unwilling to have a real relationship with me."

"Give me those," he said, taking the flowers from her. "You're making me uncomfortable."

"Good."

"Uncomfortable is good?"

He looked so confused McKenzie almost laughed.

"Absolutely."

"You've lost me."

But she hadn't. She could see it in his gorgeous eyes, in the way that they followed her every move. She really did make him uncomfortable in the most wonderful way possible.

"Don't you see, Ryder? If I made you comfortable, none of this would matter. You wouldn't be torn about your feelings for me. The past wouldn't matter in connection to me and you wouldn't have felt the need to avoid me." A light clicked. "That's always why you've avoided me. Because I'm uncomfortable."

The truth bubbled inside her. How could she not have realized?

"None of this comfortable/uncomfortable stuff matters, McKenzie. I'm not willing to have a relationship with you."

"We already have a relationship. One that started when we met and got put on hold until I asked you to go away with me."

"As your pretend boyfriend."

"The only thing pretend about that weekend was what we were telling ourselves. Everyone saw the truth, but us."

"What truth would that be?"

"That we're meant for each other."

Ryder closed his eyes and groaned. "You're here to torment me, aren't you?"

His words caused her a moment of doubt, but then she reminded herself that he was using what happened with Anna in an attempt to shut her out.

"Possibly. I had dinner with Paul last night. He wanted to get back together."

Ryder's expression darkened. "Then why are you here? With flowers?"

She moved closer to him. "I don't want to get back together with Paul. Or Clay."

* * *

The last time Ryder had bared his heart hadn't ended well.

Because the woman he'd been baring his soul to had been in love with another man.

"This isn't easy for me, either, you know?" McKenzie jabbed her finger against his chest. Would she keep doing so if she realized how each touch sent shockwaves of awareness through him?

"I've been dumped by every serious relationship I've ever been in," she continued. "Someday, you may do the same, but I've realized that someday might not ever come and wouldn't that be a beautiful thing if it didn't?"

Meaning he might not ever dump her.

"I wouldn't."

She stared up into his eyes. "Deep down I believe that, Ryder. It's why I'm here. Because, not so long ago, I thought three strikes and I was out, but in reality it's third time is the charm."

This should be easy. McKenzie was here, baring her soul to him. But old hurts cut deep.

"You can't be sure this isn't just a rebound reaction."

McKenzie laughed and shook her head. "I'm not on the rebound from Paul."

"How can you be so sure?"

"Because I was never in love with Paul. You're not the only one hiding behind walls. Part of me is terrified of being in a relationship with you because the stakes are high. I've seen what that can do to a person. I saw what it did to my mama when my daddy died."

He captured her finger poking into his chest, held it close to his heart.

"I think it's why I stayed in relationships that weren't right for me," she continued. "Because I knew that even though it would sting if they ended, which they did, it wouldn't shatter my world."

"Is that why you're here? To start another relationship that isn't right for you?"

She shook her head. "For the first time in my life, the right man is in my life. Only he isn't in my life, and that's why I'm here."

How did he explain this to her? Make her understand all the things running through his mind, through his heart?

"I have been crazy about you from the moment we met," he admitted. "Do you know how it feels to want someone so much and to know you'll never have her? That's how I felt about you right up until the day you asked me to be your pretend boyfriend."

"I didn't know. I thought you didn't like me, that I'd done something to upset you."

He snorted. "You weren't supposed to know. I didn't want you or anyone to know how I felt.

And, the only thing you did to upset me was be in a serious relationship with Paul."

"You never let on that you wanted me."

"Nor would I have had he not made the mistake of breaking things off. I'd been there, done that and planned to never get involved with another woman who was on the rebound or seriously involved with someone. Not easy when it came to you, but I managed by keeping my distance. I didn't want to like you."

"But you did anyway." She smiled as she said it, flattening her hand against his chest, covering his heart.

"Obviously."

"Not from where I was standing. I couldn't believe when you said you'd go with me to Tennessee."

"I couldn't stand the thought of you hiring an escort and possibly being taken advantage of."

"Because you thought I was on the rebound?"

"Yes."

"I am on the rebound." She stared him straight in the eyes. "From a relationship with my pretend boyfriend who stole my real heart. It's his for the taking. All he has to do is say yes."

McKenzie waited to see how Ryder would respond. Did he want her heart? Want her?

What she'd seen in his eyes had made her think

he did, but she needed to hear him say the words. Needed to know he wouldn't push her away.

"I love you, McKenzie."

Not *yes*, but she'd take those words, would take them and cherish them.

"Tell me again," she said, wrapping her arms around his neck. "Tell me over and over."

"I plan to." He kissed her, long and hard and with a possession like she'd never felt. Because she'd never been loved the way Ryder loved her. She'd never let him go, knew without doubt he'd never let her go again.

"Every day for the rest of our lives, McKenzie, I'll do more than tell you. I'll show you."

And he did.

* * * * *